Charleston Red

PRESS
Box 115, Superior, WI 54880 (715) 394-9513

ISBN Number 1-886028-58-3

Library of Congress Catalog Card Number: 2003100946

Published by:

Savage Press
P.O. Box 115
Superior, WI 54880

Phone: 715-394-9513

E-mail: mail@savpress.com

Web Site: www.savpress.com

Printed in the USA

Charleston Red

by
Sarah Galchus

To Mike & Pat:

Thank you for your
interest in my mysteries —
both real & imagined...

Fondly,
Sarah Galchus

December 2007

To

Kurt

Prologue

Afterward, Laura considered the irony. She had moved to Charleston, South Carolina, for the mystery and the romance. What she found was murder and adultery, their most malevolent reflections.

Who would have thought that autumn in the South could be so interesting?

1

L aura surveyed the Charleston rooftops from the balcony of her new home. It was September in South Carolina, and the humidity of the summer had begun to dissipate. It was a pleasure to be outdoors again.

Fort Sumter House is an eighty-year-old former hotel that, whitewashed and imposing, decorates the southernmost tip of the Charleston peninsula. It overlooks the water and Fort Sumter on one side and the rooftops of the historic district on the other. Laura's view was to the west, but with enough of a tilt that she started getting sun by noon. As a mystery novelist, she was accustomed to taking her sunlight when she could get it, occasionally staying up all night writing, but sometimes retiring early with stern plans to rise with the sun, hoping to reverse the writer's block that plagues every writer at one time or another.

On this particular morning, she had actually kept her own resolution and risen early, not because of a pledge to write, but rather to take in the excitement of her recent move to the jewel city in the Low Country's crown. Now over thirty and having published several novels, she was convinced of her talent, but spooked by a yearlong idea drought. Charleston seemed romantic, inspirational, and fresh. She relocated with very little thought—old enough to be financially secure and young enough to believe it would all turn out as it should.

So far, the city had met, even exceeded, her expectations. She had found and bought her small condo with the glorious view in a matter of days. Renovations, necessary but brief, were accomplished in several weeks. She turned from the French windows to survey her new domain.

The entire space was less than six hundred square feet. The living room was dominated by the spectacular view of the city that she was presently obscuring. To her right was a small bedroom with adjacent bath. To the left of the living room, a small oblong kitchen with a breakfast nook at its far end overlooked the balcony and the water. A wet bar connected the living room to the kitchen, and the general effect was one of spaces flowing into each other.

The seventies decor that had defined the place when she bought it was gone, having been replaced by her more modern preferences. The balcony, kitchen, and bathroom were floored in white marble. The living room and bedroom had wooden floors, and their walls were covered in textured hazelnut-hued wallpaper. Laura's interior decorator had talked her into mirrored kitchen and bath, which made the limited living space seem larger. Plants were present throughout the apartment, and a large painting of a palmetto tree scene by a local artist was strategically placed above the large leather sofa. The living room was completed by built-in floor to ceiling bookshelves, crammed with books, and a dark walnut armoire (holding the novelist's guilty pleasure, a forty- inch television) from Key West, which had been placed just to the left of the French windows leading to the balcony.

Laura stepped down into the living room to settle on the voluptuous seven-foot long sofa with her coffee. It already felt like home.

She took a long shower to celebrate the freedom of the day and decided to venture out into the fresh Saturday morning. Even in jeans and a turtleneck, she was not quite warm and was reminded again of autumn. A new Starbucks had opened several blocks away; she drove over, anticipating that additional caffeine, coupled with the crispness of *The*

Post & Courier, would generate some new ideas.

The eastern sky was pink and gold in her rearview mirror as she headed down Murray Boulevard. The waterfront homes on her right were majestic in the morning sun, but not as historic as those that existed north of White Point Gardens behind her. During her brief time in Charleston, Laura had learned that some of those homes had been part of the original battlement of the city and had even been abandoned during the Civil War as cannonballs fired from Fort Sumter had ended up in front gardens. The stately homes were well-preserved; many were on the historic registry. Their gardens dripped with blossoms year-round. Drawing rooms were often painted a deep flame color, so well-known that it was simply referred to as Charleston Red.

The streets on the eastern side of the peninsula, East Bay Street, Church Street, Meeting Street and King Street, are all interconnected by narrow, cobblestoned alleyways, giving pedestrians intriguing glimpses of secret residences tucked away from main thoroughfares. The passing centuries have lent a velvet patina to brick walls. Live oak trees hung with Spanish moss add to the charm. Palmetto trees, not indigenous to the area, are found mostly along the bigger streets where they were transplanted in the mid-twentieth century to lend a picturesque feel to a city that counts tourism as one of its major sources of revenue. Wrought iron gates and balconies are centuries old. Caribbean mingles with the European mood as most homes in this area are painted in pastel hues of pink, light blue, khaki, pale green, and marigold.

Laura wended her way through the historic district. She parked her car a block from King Street, the heart of the sophisticated shopping district, and ran over to the Starbucks coffee house. It was warm inside and smelled heavenly. The girl at the counter took her order and her money, then created a concoction of coffee, chocolate and whipped cream that looked as delicious as it smelled. Laura bought *The Post & Courier* and sank onto an aluminum café chair to begin her morning.

Two hours later it was nearing nine o'clock; she decided to head home to write.

Laura had just turned onto King Street when she spotted Kate Caxton walking near the Saks Fifth Avenue store. Dr. Katharine Porter Caxton, a retinal surgeon at Charleston Medical Center, was the first friend Laura had made in Charleston. Like many university-based hospitals, CMC had residency programs, and Laura knew Kate was probably coming home from morning rounds with one of her residents. She was dressed in taupe-colored linen pants and a black sweater, not unlike Laura's own, and her black briefcase was carelessly slung over one shoulder. Her red hair added cheery contrast to her conventional outfit. Laura detected an extra jauntiness to her step and thought she knew why. She rolled down the passenger window.

"Hey there, stranger," Laura said, pulling up alongside Kate. "The post-ops must have looked pretty good today."

Kate swung to face her, and, after a brief moment of confusion, her gaze steadied and she smiled.

"Only had two, both flat and attached," she responded, referring, as Laura now knew, to the state of her patients' retinas. "My resident this rotation is very good, punctual and thorough. All I had to do was take a quick look. He'd done everything else, and neither patient had any questions." She shrugged and tilted her head. "Makes my job a lot easier," she smiled.

Laura offered Kate a ride, although her friend's house

was just a few minutes away. "How's Mark?" Laura wondered out loud. Kate's husband of two years, Mark Caxton, was a well-known architect who had started his own successful firm, Caxton, Chivas & Ross, fifteen years ago. He and Brian Chivas were local boys who had attended Yale together. The third partner, Gigi Ross, was a highly touted city planner recruited from New York City nearly two years ago. Although Laura was still getting to know Kate, she already knew every detail of Kate and Mark's whirlwind romance. They seemed the perfect couple.

When Kate did not answer the question immediately, Laura glanced in her direction. Kate was turned away, looking west out of the window as they crossed Broad Street and headed south toward the tip of the peninsula.

Then she turned to her friend and smiled. "He's fine," she said. "They're getting excited about the Palmetto Pointe contract. Brian's in Paris to scavenge new ideas. Gigi thinks Luke is their only other rival." Luke Grimke was a powerhouse in architectural circles and well-established in Charleston despite (or maybe because of) having been brought up in the San Francisco area. "They should know by late next week."

As the two women made plans to meet for coffee the next morning, Laura turned left off King Street onto Lamont, where Kate and Mark had purchased a sprawling 1890s bungalow. It was situated on the north side of the street, thereby facing south and swathed in sunshine all day. Unlike most Charleston homes, it was set back from the street and appeared more aloof and mysterious than its taller neighbors. Its gardens were smothered in greenery; a large live oak tree was draped in silvery moss. Laura thought it was no coincidence that the picturesque property had been bought and renovated by an architect.

She dropped Kate in front of her house and watched as she disappeared through the front door. Then Laura bent to the CD player to select her music for the short drive home. She was in a Mozart mood.

Just as she was pulling away from the curb, a flash caught her eye. Turning, she saw Kate had pushed open the glassed-in front door and was staring at her. Her face was drained of all color; Laura didn't need her shaky wave to be propelled from the car and up the sidewalk. Before Kate even spoke, Laura understood that something awful had happened.

"It's Mark," Kate's voice was barely a whisper. "I think he's dead." She seemed to get a grip on herself then, perhaps remembering that she, not Laura, was the doctor. "Laura, he's dead. I think we should call the police." She seemed reluctant to go back into the house, but Laura pushed her forward, her own voice unexpectedly stern.

"Show me," Laura said. "We'll call the police as soon as we're sure."

Kate led the way down the hallway and stopped at the open door of what had been Mark's retreat from the world. Laura left her in the hall and stepped inside.

What she saw shocked her.

Mark's obviously lifeless body was lying face up across his desk. He was barefoot, dressed in khakis and what had been a white polo shirt. A large puddle of blood had pooled on his abdomen and chest and spread grotesquely onto his neck and ears and onto the surrounding desk. White paperwork and several open books were now scarlet. From there, the blood had flowed onto the floor. Laura took a step backward, trying to take in all she could, yet reluctant to stay in the room for an extra second. She saw no signs of a struggle, no bloody footprints, no murder weapon. The man was certainly dead, although recently so. Turning, she grabbed Kate and propelled her down the hallway, around the back of the stairs where a small laundry room and lavatory were creatively tucked away, and into the kitchen. She felt as though she were in slow motion, noticing everything, yet nothing at all.

Kate was sobbing silently. Settling her at the kitchen table, Laura found the phone and called 911.

Then she sat down with her friend to wait while the police came to question them about the murder of Kate's husband.

2

Kate's voice trembled as she described the start of her day to Detective Hobbs. She had a box of tissues in front of her, but the tears had stopped. Laura thought Kate was holding herself together remarkably well.

Detective Frank Hobbs seemed oblivious to her efforts. He formally began his investigation. "Dr. Caxton, please describe the events of this morning, beginning with when you got up and ending with our arrival. Be as complete as you can. We're going to tape this conversation."

Kate took a shaky breath and began.

"I operated on two patients yesterday; they had retinal detachments, so I had to go up to CMC this morning to see them. It's not unusual for me to go in on a Saturday. I have my resident see the patients, do the paperwork and go over eye drops and other postoperative requirements. That way I can come in, take a quick look, and get out of there. Sometimes there are questions that the resident is unable to answer, or maybe the patient feels better asking me, so each visit takes maybe ten minutes. If the resident also has questions, maybe fifteen. So, that's what happened this morning. I got up at six-thirty, took a quick shower and crept downstairs in my robe, so Mark could sleep." Tears threatened to fall, and the detective and Laura waited.

"I made coffee—I only like instant, and I use the microwave—and I went to the front door and got the newspaper while the coffee was in the microwave. Then I sat down for a couple minutes to read and have a little coffee. I try to walk up to the hospital, if I'm not in a hurry, so that takes about twenty minutes. I was still in my bathrobe."

She gestured to a plush, waffle-weave robe flung across the back of a chair. It looked as if it had started its life in a spa. "So I went into the laundry room and got into some clean clothes there." She hesitated. "That was so I wouldn't have to wake my husband unnecessarily; we tried to be courteous to each other that way."

"And the clothes you're wearing now are the clothes you put on then?" Detective Hobbs asked.

Kate fidgeted with her sweater. "Yes, exactly." She hesitated, as if waiting for another question, then continued. "So, I had my coffee, got dressed, got my briefcase and left the house. I left the paper out for Mark." They all looked at the far end of the table, where a newspaper had been carelessly folded together, accompanied by a clean, oversized coffee mug.

Laura remembered seeing its twin in the study, broken in half and lying on the floor.

"Okay, so what happened next?" The police officer prodded her.

"Well, I left the house by the front door and headed up King Street toward the hospital. It was a little after seven o'clock. My resident was supposed to have the post-ops ready by seven-thirty." She hesitated, then spoke in a rush. "So, I got there, saw the patients, did some paperwork and a couple dictations, then left around eight o'clock to walk home. I was almost there when I ran into Laura; she gave me a ride the rest of the way."

The detective checked his notes. "So it took you more than twice as long to walk home than it did to get there?"

Kate nodded. "Yes, I have very little time that's unstructured; it was a pleasure to be able to walk slowly and enjoy the quiet morning. It's been so nice and cool lately, I was really enjoying being outdoors." She looked at Laura as if for confirmation.

Laura nodded.

The detective continued. "What happened when you arrived at home?"

Kate closed her eyes, as if trying to see into her mind's eye. Her voice was so low that both listeners leaned forward to hear.

"I opened the door and went into the house."

"Was the door locked or unlocked?" The detective wanted to know.

"It was unlocked; we usually don't lock up unless we're going on vacation." She looked at Hobbs. "This is a very safe neighborhood."

The irony of her statement dawned immediately; all three were silent. Then Hobbs shifted position, and Kate continued her narrative.

"I immediately went into the study because that's usually where Mark is when I come home. The door was open, so I saw him right away. I didn't touch anything. I went to the front door and opened it. The sun reflected on the glass and blinded me for a second. Laura was just about to drive away, but she saw me…and came to help me." Her cold hand reached toward Laura's.

Hobbs continued to direct the narrative. "Did you notice anything unusual, something that didn't look right, or a sound or a smell that made you feel like anything was wrong?"

Kate thought about this for a moment, but slowly shook her head. "Nothing," she said. "Mark usually stayed in his study and waited for me to find him. Nothing was different except he was dead." She fixed her red-rimmed gaze on the detective, who shifted uncomfortably. "Laura agreed that he was beyond help, and we came in here to wait for you to show up." She looked down at her hands, and her auburn hair fell over her face.

The detective switched his attention to Laura. "Now, Ms. Lindross, you're new in town, aren't you?" He made it sound like the eighth deadly sin.

Although she could not see how that mattered, Laura nodded. "I moved here in August. Kate was one of the first people I met. We ran into each other jogging on the Battery and became friends."

At Hobbs' request, she detailed her morning, finishing with his arrival at the front door. Like Kate, she was unable to put her finger on anything that had seemed out of place. She had not spent much time in the Caxton house, but all was as she remembered it.

Hobbs clicked off the tape recorder just as his partner came into the room.

"The coroner's done with the body, and they're gonna transport it to the morgue," Detective Jeff Marcus quietly reported. He did not want to upset the women in the room any further. "Photography and fingerprints are done too. We're gonna have to check the house next."

Kate and Laura were instructed to remain at the kitchen table and not to touch anything. They were not allowed to use the telephone. The small downstairs bathroom was meticulously photographed and dusted for fingerprints before they were allowed to use it. Under the watchful gaze of a young police officer, the women did not speak much. Two hours later, they were asked further questions.

"Tell me about anyone who might have done this, Doctor," Hobbs' voice was smooth. "Did your husband have any enemies that you know of?"

A shadow of a smile flashed over Kate's face, perhaps disbelief at being asked such a melodramatic question. "No, he had no enemies, Detective," she said. "He was a successful businessman. I'm sure there were people who didn't like him, but I doubt anyone was angry enough to kill him. He got along well with his two partners, Brian Chivas, a friend since childhood, and Gigi Ross. I know there's a high- profile contract regarding the Palmetto Pointe project that his firm and another architect were vying for. But I find it hard to believe..."

"Which firm is that?" Hobbs asked, pen poised over his notebook.

"Grimke & Associates, on Meeting Street," Kate said. "They were the major competitor of my husband's company—Caxton, Chivas & Ross. But I actually think all parties concerned had a great deal of respect for one another."

"Anyone else who may have wished your husband ill?"

Kate seemed to think for a moment, then spoke slowly. "My husband was a sweet guy, Detective, as well as successful and good looking," she said. "I know that when I married him, there were some disappointed women out there. They probably disliked me more than him, however, especially more than two years after the fact."

"Tell me about that."

She seemed reluctant to name anyone in particular, but Hobbs persisted.

"Well, Mark didn't talk about his previous relationships much, Detective, as you can imagine, but I know that Amanda Michaels, the gallery owner, was surprised when he left her to marry me. But I've never heard an unkind word about her. She certainly has been nothing but civil to me on the few occasions that we've run into each other." Laura knew Kate felt bad about the unchivalrous way in which Mark had ended his relationship with Amanda, but she had always said that was his business and not hers. "Amanda is the business partner of Brian's wife, Melanie Moore Chivas. Their gallery, Michaels & Moore Gallery, is located on East Bay Street. Melanie's a good friend of mine, too, so Amanda and I sometimes see each other in public. I've never been uncomfortable with that."

Hobbs seemed to grasp the situation. "So, your husband really had no enemies that you know of?"

Slowly, Kate shook her head. "No."

* * * * *

"Michaels & Moore Gallery," Melanie's tone was light as she picked up the telephone. Although it was nearly noon, the day seemed to be progressing slowly and peacefully, and she was only on her second cup of coffee. Since her business partner, Amanda Michaels, was no longer a coffee drinker, a whole glorious pot of hazelnut java was hers if she wanted it.

"Oh, hi, Kate." As she listened to the voice at the other end of the line, Melanie's face changed. Amanda, working at a canvas at the far end of the studio, straightened up, aware that something was wrong. A lithe, brown-eyed blonde, she put down her paintbrush and strained to hear the conversation, then quietly came to stand at the desk next to her friend.

Amanda could not remember a time when she had not been fascinated by watercolor. By the time she was in grade school, her gift was obvious, and a friend of her mother's had permitted the little girl to display paintings in her gallery. Amanda had sold her first painting when she was eight years old; the surprised buyer had become a lifelong friend. Amanda had been away from her native Charleston for six years, returning only after her studies in Atlanta were complete. She had missed the city whose magic, she felt, was best captured in watercolor. Many other artists agreed with her; art galleries became a popular business in the city, along with antique stores and restauranteuring. Amanda soon decided to open a gallery and realized that a partner would be necessary to enable her to paint, run a business, and pay the bills.

She met Melanie Moore in a cafe one day. Melanie was trying to persuade the owner to display her paintings. Also a native Charlestonian, Melanie was brought up in the affluence of lower Meeting Street, where her talent was not encouraged. When Melanie prioritized her interest in art over that of being a debutante, her family supported her, but grudgingly. Melanie did not go to college or receive any formal training. She didn't need it. She preferred charcoal sketches, but had such a good eye that everything she tried was impressive.

She and Amanda became good friends.

They soon signed a lease for a small gallery space on the second floor of an old meat-packaging factory on East Bay Street. The cavernous building had been split into three levels a decade ago and bisected vertically. Residential spaces were on the south side, while the spaces with northern light were more appropriate for business endeavors. The ground floor housed an expensive boutique that never seemed to do any substantial business, but, nevertheless, had been open for nearly a decade. Amanda thought that a large part of the business for their gallery came from the boutique's wealthy clientele. The top floor was a second-hand bookstore with a small coffee bar, one that Amanda and Melanie themselves frequented, as much for the relaxing atmosphere and view of the harbor as for the excellent selection of books.

As Amanda waited for Melanie to get off the telephone, she glanced around the gallery.

She was proud of it. Her calm temperament and love of color had been infused into the space. Honey-colored wooden floors ran along the entire length of the room, which was seventy feet long and twenty feet wide. A spiral staircase had been fitted into the floor centrally. A second spiral stair, at the back of the gallery, afforded an additional entrance, this one from the quaint cobblestone alleyway that ran along the north side of the building, connecting East Bay to State Street. The south wall, windowless, was a warm pinky-gold color. Like a good nude lipstick that goes with everything, this created a neutral palette for the paintings, each one lit by an ornate sconce light. Large windows were thoughtfully spaced on the north wall. Additional dividers split the room into pleasant niches with plenty of room to display the artwork that had made the Michaels & Moore Gallery famous.

Amanda leaned against the polished surface of the crescent-shaped desk and tried to decipher the conversation. After a startled disclaimer of "Oh my God! No! What happened?" Melanie's end of the conversation consisted mostly of intermittent murmurs that sounded sympathetic and stunned all at once. It did not seem to occur to her to meet Amanda's gaze until she finally said, "Of course, I'll be right there. Three minutes." Then she put down the telephone and looked at Amanda.

"That was Kate Caxton," she said. "Mark's dead." Melanie's brown eyes were sympathetic as she watched her friend. She knew that Amanda and Mark had a long history together. "He was apparently stabbed to death in his study early this morning, unbelievable as that sounds. The police have been and gone, and Kate wants me to come over there." Melanie reached in and gave Amanda a hug. "I'm sorry, honey, are you going to be all right?"

Amanda nodded, feeling curiously empty inside. "Absolutely, you go be with Kate. I'll stay here, it's been slow today, and I was late getting in anyway." She sat down at the bar stool behind the desk, seemingly unaware of Melanie's concerned glance.

A few moments later, however, as she watched her friend vanish down the spiral staircase that led to the alley, Amanda's face crumpled, and she sobbed.

3

Melanie descended into the alley and hurried toward State Street.

She remembered the cold February day several years ago when Mark had first walked into their lives. It had actually snowed that day, a rarity in Charleston. She and Amanda had watched happy children squealing on the gray slate pavement outside their gallery. The kids' delight had been infectious; when Mark showed up they'd been giggling like a couple of schoolgirls. He had come to buy a painting for his newly renovated office. The inclement weather kept other patrons away; the three of them had bonded over cups of hot cocoa while enjoying the task of selecting the perfect painting. Mark's attraction to Amanda had been obvious immediately, and he had promised Melanie a date with his best friend, a childhood pal who was now his business partner, a guy named Brian.

The next night they had all gone out to Saracen's, a nearby restaurant.

Melanie had immediately felt that night was special. The unique Moorish facade of the building had been analyzed by many art historians and gave no hint that the building had originally housed a bank. Inside, the space was most reminiscent of a church; the low lighting and hushed tones of the other patrons had heightened the ecclesiastical feel. They ended the evening upstairs, at Charlie's Little Bar, having drinks and cigars, talking and laughing. Melanie realized she liked Brian more than anyone she had dated in recent memory; their wedding eighteen months later surprised no one.

Mark and Amanda had seemed poised on the brink of marriage as well. Until Kate.

A car honked; Melanie was abruptly pulled back into the present. She crossed Broad Street and hurried toward King. The midday bustle of the business district usually invigorated her, but things were subdued on a Saturday. She hurried past the facade of Caxton, Chivas & Ross, its dark windows watching her. After Mark had started dating Kate, whom he had met when he was chief architect for a renovation of the hospital wing where she worked, Amanda had been devastated. Although she claimed to have gotten over him with no hard feelings, Melanie knew she had not dated anyone seriously in the three years since.

Several minutes later, Melanie crossed the sidewalk to the Caxton house. Kate and Laura were waiting for her.

Laura had met Melanie on one other occasion, about a month previously. She and Kate were taking a break from a rare day of shopping at the various stores in Charleston Place and on King Street. They had finished up at Nine West and were intending to browse at the Body Shop next when they realized they were ravenous. Heading to Fulton Five, a long-time Charleston landmark, tucked in, predictably, at the eastern end of Fulton Street, they were soon settled in at the Italian restaurant, red wine in front of them and linguine on the way. Suddenly assaulted by color, noise, and motion, Laura observed a short, slender woman with lively eyes and curly black hair bearing down on them with coos of delight. In her wake was a solidly-built, good-looking man, an indulgent smile hovering on his lips.

"Kate, honey, how're you doing?" The woman's southern accent was pronounced. "Brian and I were just talking about how you work too hard and play too little! And now here you are, doing some shopping! Without your husband, I see. Always the best way!" She glanced appreciatively at their multiple bags and boxes and smiled at Laura. "I don't believe we've met."

Kate made the introductions. "Brian and Melanie Chivas, meet my friend, Laura Lindross. Laura, this is my husband's business partner, Brian, and his wife Melanie."

"Nice to meet you," Laura said. She had heard plenty about how kind Melanie had been to Kate in the early days of her relationship with Mark, while Brian's allegiance lay completely with Amanda. "I understand you two are Charleston born and bred. You must be proud of your city."

Melanie edged into the booth next to her while Brian signaled the waiter for a drink. "Seven and seven, please. Sweetie, anything for you?" Melanie ordered a glass of wine, and they made themselves comfortable, Brian's arm around Kate, clearly assuming they were welcome. Kate smiled at Laura and winked, while Melanie, who had actually read one of Laura's books, began to cross-examine her about her life as a mystery novelist.

"Yes," Laura replied to a commonly asked question. "I always knew I'd write a book. My first one was sloshing around in my head for years before I actually got a computer and wrote it down. It almost wrote itself, in fact." Laura had completed her first book in four months, a therapeutic process after an unpleasant break-up with a guy she had been seeing. Knowing the kind of man he was, she was sure he would insist on royalties if he ever learned of his pivotal role in her entry into the world of publishing. "I've had a bit of a dry spell recently and moved to Charleston last month to try to generate some fresh ideas."

Melanie tilted her head and smiled at her husband. Her rosebud mouth and raven hair were in sharp contrast to her milky skin, and Laura could see her affection reflected in his eyes. Though she was so petite and he so large, they seemed to fit well together. Laura guessed this relationship was built on similarity of spirit and mutual respect.

"Sweetie, don't we have a few Charleston scandals to get her mind working?"

Brian furrowed his brow and suggested a historical novel interweaving a good old-fashioned murder mystery with the many stories of Charleston's ghosts. Laura listened, entranced, as he related several ghost stories; even Kate and Melanie, who had heard the tales before, stopped eating during the more lurid bits. "My favorite is the story of Mary, a ghost who haunts the Unitarian cemetery on King Street looking for her husband. He died in Baltimore; his body was never returned to Charleston. Although she died on the same day in 1907, she's been looking for him ever since."

When her husband stopped talking, Melanie smiled and clapped her hands. "Honey, very good, maybe you could be a guide for the Ghost Tour if architecture ever falls through. You're perfect!"

Lunch passed quickly, with Melanie's energy and positiveness pervading the conversation. Laura could see why she was Kate's best friend. She had a knack for making people feel good about themselves.

As she came to Kate's door today, Melanie knew she had her work cut out for her. Kate wrapped her arms around her friend and was herded into the kitchen where Laura boiled water while Melanie gently began to ask questions. Trying to answer them, Kate soon became calmer and drank the tea Laura brought to the table.

"Do you have any idea at all what might have led up to this? Kate, even little things are important. Think!" Melanie implored her friend.

"I have no idea at all who did this to him," Kate returned. "It's very unreal, like a slowly evolving nightmare. One minute I almost feel okay, and then it hits me that he's gone." She began to sniffle just as the phone rang. Laura tried to remember if Mark had parents or siblings who would have to be notified.

Melanie picked it up. "Caxton residence," she said, cautiously eyeing her crying friend. Clearly, she was concerned that Kate was not fit to break the tragic news to anyone. A moment later, relief was evident on her face.

"Hi, Gigi," she said. "Yes, it's true, I didn't know it was on the news already, but I'm with her right now. The police just left." She listened for a while; Laura guessed her conversation was with Gigi Ross, the third partner in the firm, who seemed to be expressing disbelief about Mark's death and concern over Kate's well-being. "No, I haven't told Brian yet, he's still in Paris, he's coming back tomorrow night." A sigh. "No, I'll call him later, he'll understand that it's been chaos. In fact, after I pick him up at the airport, our first stop will probably be the Harris Teeter grocery to do shopping I should have done days ago." She smiled faintly, and, after a final brief exchange, hung up the phone.

"Thanks for getting that," Kate spoke to her friend gratefully. "I really don't want to talk. Gigi's more of an acquaintance than a friend, but it was nice of her to call." She turned to look at the other woman. "Laura, you've been such a doll, staying here with me all morning. You probably need to go take a breather, I'll be okay."

Melanie nodded, and she and Laura left Kate in the kitchen and moved into the sunlit living room. Maroon and navy Persian rugs interspersed with green and cream were soft underfoot. A classic Henry Kloss radio poured out a soft wash of Schubert, and Laura recognized one of her favorites, the "Trout Quintet." The two women walked past several retro egg chairs upholstered in dense cotton chenille. These matched the two large sofas, but would have been impressive all on their own as well. Laura knew she was not the only one who thought Arne Jacobsen was a genius. The big screen television was dark. The sunlight that poured into the living room through two arched doorways from the glass-roofed sun room on the west side of the house seemed obscenely cheerful.

"I'll stay with her for a while," Melanie whispered as she showed Laura out the front door.

In the end, Laura left, not because she had things to do, but because she saw Detectives Hobbs and Marcus emerge from their squad car and walk up to the door of the three-story row house across the street.

* * * * *

Laura found out later exactly how the conversation with the neighbor, Bill Sullivan, had gone.

Having recently shattered his foot by dropping a large trestle while renovating his attic, Bill was now laid up for several weeks and spent a good part of his time trying to alleviate the boredom by watching activities on the street below the window of his second story bedroom. His chair of choice for this activity was a large La-Z-Boy littered with car racing magazines and dog hair. His two very large rottweilers, Jake and Jasmine, were dutifully camping out at his feet, although they must have been dying for a run, or, at least, an excursion around the block.

"And what, if anything, did you see from your, uh, vantage point this morning between seven and nine o'clock?" Hobbs asked. Bill knew Mark had been murdered, but did not know much else.

He seemed to consider the question. "Well, I woke up

at seven or so, when the dogs started bugging me to be fed. By maybe seven-twenty I had coffee and was sitting down with the newspaper." He stopped and then shrugged. "I didn't really see anything until I saw the doctor walk up to the door and go inside. I never saw her leave. Then I must have dozed off; the next thing I remember is the dogs barking because the squad cars were pulling up out front."

Hobbs was quite still. "You saw Dr. Caxton come up her sidewalk and go into the house?"

"Yeah," Bill seemed unimpressed at delivering this piece of information.

"What time was this?" Marcus asked.

"Must've been before seven forty-five, because the clock chimed the three-quarter hour shortly after that." He motioned at an antique clock on the mantel of the fireplace. "I remember thinking that her patients must have looked good because she was home earlier than usual. No scrubs, either, she was in khakis and a sweater. Black, I think."

Hobbs attempted to recap in a steady voice. "You got to the window at seven-twenty, read for a while and had coffee, noticed Dr. Caxton entering her house at seven forty-five, saw no one else on the street, then fell asleep, awaking to find police cars in the street below?"

Bill nodded, then paused. "Well, I actually saw one other person going by, before the doctor, a guy in shorts and a t-shirt. He looked like he was about to start jogging. Walked right by the house and disappeared out of my line of view." He shifted, a bit uncomfortably. "Mind you now, I can't be sure no one else passed, I was reading, mostly, and went down once to get more coffee."

4

L uke Grimke was golfing on Kiawah Island. He had driven too fast down Maybank Highway, relishing the feel of his new Jaguar convertible at full throttle in the alternating light and shadow created by the sun streaming through the canopy of live oaks hung with Spanish moss. Catching glimpses of white-pillared plantation houses, he could smell the scent of the sea. He felt he was breathing in the quintessence of the South.

Luke was desperate to escape to the golf course, where everything slowed down for him and made sense. He did not like to admit how much stress he was under with the Palmetto Pointe contract. It was a big one; other businesses, not to mention wealthy clients, would take their cue directly from the decisions made by the Palmetto Pointe executive board. Although Luke was no longer challenged by designing townhouse complexes, he still wanted to design Palmetto Pointe. On the eastern side of the peninsula, off East Bay Street, it would complement the new aquarium and cater to the family-oriented professionals who were moving to town. Ansonborough was becoming more revitalized every year. In the sixties, it had still been a ghetto.

"Good morning, Mr. Grimke," the guard at the exclusive resort greeted him. Luke was pleased to note that it was not yet nine o'clock. He expected some quiet time on the golf course by himself.

The Ocean Course, as always, worked its magic. Perhaps because he had grown up in the San Francisco Bay area, Luke always felt best within sight of the ocean. He loved the fingers of marshland that made this golf course one of the most stunning in the world. Herons stood immobile in the early morning sun. The only sound was the dull roar of the sea and the occasional call of a sea gull.

Luke was content.

After completing eighteen holes, he put his feet up in the clubhouse. He unwound with a bourbon and water and was contemplating a nap when his solitude was rudely interrupted.

"Mr. Luke Grimke?" He opened one eye and sat up abruptly. Two police officers were standing next to his club chair. He got to his feet.

"Yes, may I help you?" Luke was aware of the puzzled gaze of the only other person in the room and discreetly led the officers through French doors onto the terrace. The view of the Atlantic was comforting.

Detective Hobbs kept a keen eye on the architect. He saw an athletic man of approximately fifty, wearing a sapphire polo shirt, khakis and golf shoes, with distinguished flecks of gray in his still thick hair. With his Paul Newman eyes and a healthy tan, Luke looked every inch the astute and wealthy professional he was. Hobbs wondered if he was married.

"Mr. Grimke, I regret to inform you that Mark Caxton died this morning. He was an acquaintance of yours, is that correct?"

Grimke looked pale underneath his tan. "Good Lord, man, Mark Caxton? Dead? He was barely forty! What the hell happened to him?" He stared at Hobbs, who answered the question.

"Stabbed? Stabbed to death? I can't believe it." Luke stood up and walked to the edge of the terrace. "I'm having difficulty taking it in, Detective." He stood for a moment surveying the ocean, then returned to the wrought iron table and dropped heavily into a cushioned chair. After a deep breath, he appeared calmer.

"Of course I knew him, we were both architects in town, in Charleston, had a sort of friendly rivalry over the last decade or so. I have the highest opinion of him." He didn't seem to notice his use of the present tense. "Is there a particular question you have for me?"

"Mr. Grimke, it's nice of you to speak with us. We are simply asking some questions of many people who knew the deceased." Hobbs spoke slowly. "Can you tell us where you were between seven and eight-thirty this morning?"

Luke did not seem affronted by the question and took a moment before responding. "Well, I got up at about seven o'clock and took a jog on the Battery," he explained. "Got back to the house around seven-thirty and sat down with the paper. Decided on Kiawah for a little golf today and hit the road around eight-thirty. Got here before nine, guard can tell you that. Drove a bit too fast, I'm afraid." He had the grace to look abashed.

"Are you married, Mr. Grimke?" Marcus asked the question.

"I suppose you're wondering if there's anyone who can vouch for my whereabouts this morning," Luke commented without rancor. "No, I've never had the pleasure."

* * * * *

"Good afternoon, welcome to the gallery." Amanda's pale skin flushed as she looked at the police officers on the other side of the desk. "May I help you?"

"I'm Detective Frank Hobbs of the Charleston Police Department. This is my partner, Detective Jeff Marcus. We're attempting to locate Mr. Brian Chivas for questioning in relation to a police matter. I understand his wife works here," Hobbs continued. "Perhaps Mrs. Chivas could call us at her earliest convenience with his whereabouts or re-lay the message to her husband."

Amanda decided to let Melanie tell the police Brian was in Paris until tomorrow night. "Certainly, I'll pass it along. I expect her back momentarily."

"We also want to ask a few questions of Ms. Amanda Michaels." Hobbs thought he probably was speaking to her. "Is she available?"

"I'm Amanda," she said, extending her hand to him. She did not make eye contact with the other detective. After handshakes and a quick visual scan around the gallery to ensure privacy, the threesome sat down in the small office behind the desk. "How can I help you?"

Marcus noticed that, although Amanda's hands were motionless in her lap, her knuckles were white. He proceeded with the bad news. "Mr. Mark Caxton, a prominent local architect with whom I believe you once had a relationship, has been found dead. Can you tell us when you last saw Mr. Caxton?"

Amanda did not reply immediately. She seemed to be struggling with what to say. Finally, she raised her eyes to his and spoke. "Detective, it would be dishonest of me if I were to express surprise over your news. Kate Caxton already called the gallery about three hours ago to tell us about Mark. Melanie has gone over to the house to be with her for a while." She sighed. "Yes, I knew Mark, very well, in fact. We dated for about two years, almost got married." She shook her head. "It's been several years, but I'm still stunned and extremely saddened by the news."

The police officers waited; Amanda continued. "I last saw him about three days ago. I was locking up the gallery, and he was walking down East Bay toward the Old Exchange, on the other side of the street. I waved, and he waved back, but we didn't speak. I believe he was with Kate."

"Do you know Dr. Caxton well?"

Amanda's smile appeared to be genuine. "Not as well as I would like. We've met, on occasion, and she seems, much as I hate to admit it, the perfect match for Mark. It was hard on me when they got together, but everything happens for a reason. I've made my peace with that." She paused. "Actually, I think Mark was more uncomfortable with the situation than either of us. Sometimes he seemed to go out of his way to prevent us from meeting. I mean, Melanie is my business partner, and she's also Kate's best friend. It would have made sense for the group of us to get together socially now and then."

"Where were you between seven o'clock and eight-thirty this morning, Ms. Michaels?"

Amanda didn't hesitate. "Our gallery opens at seven-thirty on Saturdays from April through September, Detective, tourist season, you know. We like to get in a little before that to prepare for the day."

The telephone rang as Hobbs and Marcus were leaving the gallery. It was Melanie. The news of Brian's return from Paris late Sunday night was passed along. Hobbs nodded. "We'll be questioning him first thing on Monday morning."

* * * * *

Gigi Ross had been expecting the police officers who rang her doorbell shortly after four o'clock. She had dressed accordingly.

Her brick home with black shutters on the eastern end of Wentworth Street was reminiscent of the classy

Georgetown homes in Washington, D.C., where she had grown up as the only daughter of a Pentagon official. After graduate school in architecture, she had moved to New York City and established a reputation as a young professional who would stop at nothing to get what she wanted. Gigi threw herself into her work, so her various relationships with eligible men, some many years older than she, were inevitably short-lived as her career took center stage. In her male-dominated profession, most men admired her and viewed her as one of themselves.

Despite her enviable life-style, as she neared forty, Gigi found herself wanting a change. She had once spent a secret weekend at a small bed and breakfast in Beaufort, South Carolina, with a married lover, and although he soon disappeared from her life, Gigi's fascination with the South grew. She dreamed of old oak trees and antebellum homes, mint juleps and romantic walks on the beach at night.

When she discovered that her father's paternal grandmother had come from Charleston, she took this as a sign. Several months later, on glancing through *Architectural Review*, Gigi saw the advertisement placed by the Caxton & Chivas firm. She knew the job was hers before she even went for the interview. The South was in her blood, and she would find herself there.

That day she had worn a conservative brown tweed suit that set off her russet-colored hair. The skirt was a bit short and the heels a bit high, but Gigi knew how to work female attributes in her favor in a male-dominated world.

Today, she still favored striking color, but was in a violet dressing gown with matching mules. She feigned surprise at seeing the policemen and invited them in.

After offering drinks, which Hobbs and Marcus refused, she poured herself a wine spritzer. "What can I do for you gentlemen?" She inquired, a trifle breathlessly. "I assume this is in relation to Mark's death. I saw it on the news and called Kate right away. She seems to be holding up quite well."

Hobbs and Marcus exchanged glances and got to the point. "When did you last see Mr. Caxton?"

"Oh, now, honey," Gigi smiled, "you can't be serious. Of course I last saw him at work last night. We were having a powwow about the Palmetto Pointe contract and did a conference call with Brian in Paris around six o'clock. Brian has some good ideas, and we were all excited because the only other real competition is Luke Grimke; he's done the townhouse theme to death, no more fresh ideas there."

As Gigi continued to speak about her vision for the enclave, it was clear why she had accomplished so much in her field. Her love for architecture and innovation shone through her words.

"We called it a night after that. Mark dropped me here, then I assume he went home." She paused. "Of course, from what I hear, that wife-doctor of his is never at home, so he may well have gone elsewhere, but far be it from me to hypothesize."

If Hobbs noticed her thinly-veiled malice, he did not pursue it. "Ms. Ross, where were you between seven and eight-thirty this morning?"

Gigi suddenly became serious. "Well, I always get up at six o'clock to walk my dog, and today wasn't an exception. He's a Kuvasz," she offered by way of explanation, although the detectives had already noticed the large, silent, snowy white dog patiently sitting at his mistress's feet. "By seven-thirty I was downtown at the new Metropolitan store on King Street, browsing. They're having a two-day sale; I wanted to be there as soon as they opened. I spent a lot of money, I'm afraid." She smiled and indicated a large moss-colored chenille afghan, bottle-green martini glasses, several beautiful silver picture frames and a hanging lamp blown of opaque amber-colored glass decorated with wrought iron detail that must have cost several hundred dollars. Several other knick-knacks were apparent as well. "I stayed until midmorning and got home just in time to see the news of Mark's death on TV." The joy abruptly left her face.

Hobbs made a note of the store's name and King Street address. Then he looked up, hoping to appeal to Gigi's obvious intelligence. "Ms. Ross, you were very close to the deceased. Was there anything bothering him in recent days, anything that he seemed worried about or preoccupied with?"

Gigi shook her head. "Nothing except the Palmetto Pointe contract. That was consuming pretty much everyone's attention. If there was anything else he was worried about, I didn't sense it. He certainly told me nothing."

"Do you know anyone at all who may have wished to harm him?"

Gigi's tone was light. "Well, now, didn't Agatha Christie always say to look at the spouse first?"

5

Brian Chivas tried to ignore the appreciative glance of the attractive Parisienne who seated herself at the adjacent table.

Like many French women, this one had an air of self-confidence and an easy familiarity with fashion. Her graceful figure drew the attention of several other patrons in the small outdoor cafe. Brian kept his gaze on the bustling Champs-Elysées and felt, rather than saw, long legs crossing thigh over thigh under a short navy blue dress. He had no difficulty identifying her throaty voice amidst the din of the other diners.

"Campari et soda, s'il vous plait," she purred.

It was nearly ten o'clock at night, but the Champs-Elysées remained crowded with tourists, businessmen, and the native French, who gathered in small groups in the scattered cafes, drinking red wine, talking, touching, laughing in the way that only the French can. Brian could pick out the other Americans, the businessmen sitting alone with a newspaper or contemplative gaze, the tired families on vacation, determined to have fun during the much-awaited trip abroad.

He had spent nearly a week in the City of Light and enjoyed it as much as every other trip. Cigarette smoke wafted over the moist evening air, and laughter spattered the night.

It had been his idea to infuse their townhouse proposal with a French theme, linking pied-à-terre with European elegance. Ansonborough already had a European feel to it; their proposal would augment the impression of old Charleston and tie the new enclave in with the established port city. Gigi had been the one to suggest that he actually fly to Paris to absorb the atmosphere for a week, taking plenty of photographs to expedite the completion of the blueprints that Caxton, Chivas & Ross were already preparing.

Brian reflected that Gigi really was every bit as brilliant as her resume had suggested two years ago. She was a great asset to their firm. Her personal life might leave some things to be desired, but she certainly did not let the drama there interfere with her ability to do her job.

He finished his dinner, including a half-bottle of excellent Gevrey Chambertin, and waved over the garcon for coffee. This was delivered to him; he added cream and even some sugar. Despite the lateness of the hour, he took an appreciative sip. He was not worried about not being able to sleep. The jet lag would screw up his circadian rhythm anyway, and he wanted to enjoy his last night in Paris. He watched some uniformed sailors trying to pick up two well-dressed girls and was riveted by an elegant pink-haired woman striding down the street with what looked like a large muscular dog but on closer inspection appeared to be a small wildcat, a puma perhaps, on a studded leash. Brian shook his head, reflecting on the uproar this would create in the United States. He had recently read an article about a farm in Texas for wildcats and was well aware of the controversy this was causing. It would probably go all the way to the Supreme Court. Europe certainly was different from the United States, Brian reflected, freer perhaps, more whimsical, less restrictive.

As if reading his mind, the woman at the adjacent table spoke in his ear. Her accent was charming. "Excusez-moi, would you happen to have a light?" Her slender hand, the nails polished fire engine red, held a small gauloise, and her inquiring gaze, not that innocent, met his.

"Mais, oui." Brian's French was quite good; the woman's very red lips curved into an appreciative smile.

Her eyes followed his as he lit her cigarette and then lit one of his own. He rarely smoked at home, as Melanie didn't care for it, but, somehow, here, it seemed like the thing to do. He reflected for a moment on the prominence of smoking and rich foods in France. Kate had once said that the only reason the French didn't all die prematurely of heart attacks was because they offset their coronary artery disease by their equal enthusiasm for alcohol consumption. That was her personal as well her professional opinion, she'd said. She had once dated a French guy, Brian remembered, during a semester abroad, and should know.

Briefly, he wondered how that relationship had ended. He had a feeling that his best friend's wife had lived a little before settling down.

Thinking of Kate and Mark, Brian sighed and realized that the woman at the next table was speaking to him. He brushed off thoughts of home and allowed himself to be drawn in by his attractive dinner companion. When they finished their coffee, he paid both tabs. She took his arm possessively as they left the restaurant.

They window-shopped and talked. He told her he was an architect returning to the United States the next day. She was the recently divorced owner of a Chanel boutique nearby. Brian found himself enjoying the company of a beautiful woman as much as any red-blooded American male, but when they arrived at her apartment, he declined her inevitable invitation. Anger shone for a moment in her green cat eyes, then she nodded.

"I see how it is," she said. "You are one of the few who actually loves his wife. She must be quite something, that woman. Eh bien, I wish you a safe trip back to her, mon ami. Bon voyage."

Her words were still echoing in his thoughts when he unlocked his hotel room at the Georges Cinq. He noted the bedspread turned back and the chilled wine by the window. A fire burned in the grate.

Brian stepped over to the window, where the city lay below him, and thought about an additional glass of wine. It never seemed to affect him as it did others. He had never been hung over, and, like most men, he had vowed never to sleep with another woman while he was married to his wife. Not that he didn't fantasize, but they had a bond of trust. Temptation did not flow strongly in his veins.

Brian stepped away from the window, stripped off his clothes, and headed for the shower. He was a big man, well-muscled with a healthy tan coloring his skin. He and Melanie had been out on the boat just last weekend. He grinned, remembering their impromptu lovemaking on the Ashley River as the sun sank on the horizon. Stepping into the black marble shower, he availed himself of the pastel-hued shampoo and conditioner, then used the small bar of soap emblazoned with the hotel logo. The water was hot, and the jet was strong. The soap smelled like a summer day. Life was good, Brian reflected, and staying in a first-rate hotel certainly had its benefits. He stepped from the shower and grabbed a plush towel, pulling it carelessly around his waist. He was just considering calling for a pre-bed massage when the telephone rang.

"Chivas here," he spoke abruptly.

"Hi honey," Melanie's voice made him smile, but she sounded funny. "How's Paris?"

"It's fine, sweetheart, how are you?" He felt her hesitate. "Is something wrong?"

Melanie took a deep breath. "Brian, there's no good way to tell you this. There's been an ... accident. Mark's dead."

There was silence on the other end of the line as Brian tried to assimilate the news. His world exploded. "Dead? Mark? I can't believe it, what happened? Does this have anything to do with—?" He stopped himself, remembering a promise to a friend. His wife was not the person to tell about this.

Melanie missed his hesitation. "They don't know yet, exactly. Kate and that novelist friend of hers found him early this morning. Apparently he was actually stabbed to death. They don't know who did it."

"You mean someone killed him? He was murdered?" Brian sat down heavily on the edge of the bed.

"Yes," Melanie's voice was small. "Honey, are you okay? I can't even believe it myself."

Brian was quiet for a moment. "Well, I'll be home tomorrow, I think I arrive at eight-forty tomorrow night." He looked for the itinerary that Cleo Cooper, the office secretary, had tucked in with his passport before he left. "They'll find whoever did it. How's Kate holding up?" he asked, as an apparent afterthought.

"She's okay, actually," Melanie said. "She's staying here tonight; we're going to stay up and talk, maybe watch a movie to take her mind off things. There's a James Bond retrospective on TV." Melanie smiled. Kate's predilection for Sean Connery was well known.

"Sounds like you've got a plan," Brian said, wishing, as he got off the telephone, that the same could be said for himself.

The next afternoon, after a sleepless night, Brian sat in an airport bar at Charles DeGaulle, absently swirling a scotch on the rocks and remembering his best friend. *It'll be a dark day in hell if I ever get my hands on the bastard who killed him,* he vowed. *No one deserves to die like this. And he had everything going for him...*

They had been friends forever. For some reason, Brian's thoughts went back to a warm spring day in Charleston when they had been maybe eleven or twelve, in the sixth grade. On the brink of discovering girls, they had still been captivated by the two golden retriever strays they had encountered one day while coming home from school.

"You want to take them home? Do you think we can?" Brian had asked his friend.

"Sure," Mark stated, expansive in his certainty, even though his family already had two dogs at home. The plump puppies were hard to resist; each boy had scooped up a dog, making plans to train them together and have a loyal friend for life. *Or at least for a few weeks that summer,* Brian thought wryly. His dog, Sammy, had been a well-loved priority until he died the summer Brian had started graduate school. Mark's dog, Chief, had soon joined the passel of other dogs in the Caxton household, as Mark fell in love with an expensive German shepherd, complete with certificate of breeding.

The same thing happened with Kate all those months ago, Brian realized. *He found something new that captured a different side of his enthusiasms and had to have it. But you could never hate him for it, that's just the way he was...*

Brian's thoughts were interrupted by the boarding announcement for his flight.

"Ladies and gentlemen, Delta Airlines announces the boarding of Flight 8250 to Atlanta, Georgia, U. S. A. Now boarding at Gate 12, Flight 8250 to Atlanta, Georgia." The announcement was repeated in French. "Messieurs et mesdames..."

Brian finished his drink, got off the bar stool and walked to the gate.

Tucked into the last seat of the first class cabin a few

minutes later, he asked for a bourbon and water, which was presented to him in a tall glass with an embossed napkin. He stowed his briefcase under the seat in front of him, knowing that as soon as the aircraft reached cruising altitude, he would be able to bring out his laptop and finalize his impressions of the Palmetto Pointe enclave. He felt the trip had been successful. Then he remembered Mark. It didn't really matter now.

Brian received a second drink and drained it, leaning back and closing his eyes. The chaos around him gradually became a dull roar. He was pleased to note that there were no screaming children in his vicinity. The 747 began to move, slowly at first, then faster.

"Ladies and gentlemen, we are third in line for takeoff. We anticipate a smooth flight today over the Atlantic to Atlanta, Georgia. We thank you for choosing Delta Airlines and hope you will sit back and enjoy the flight."

6

Sunday morning in Charleston was unexpectedly warm. Melanie awoke with a feeling of dread in the pit of her stomach that she could not immediately place. It took her a moment to remember yesterday's events.

In retrospect, she was shocked anew and wondered that she had even been able to sleep at all. Pulling back the pale pink flannel sheets she liked to use when Brian was away on business, she moved softly across the room and opened the door. The dark, polished wooden floor of the hallway stretched before her. She grabbed her robe and made her way down the hallway, trying to be quiet as she passed the guest room where Kate slept.

Tiptoeing down the steep staircase, she entered the kitchen. It was lit with early morning sun, and the pale yellow walls were suffused with golden color.

Melanie went over to the sink and washed out the coffee pot. She placed the pre-ground coffee beans into the filter, added water and, flipping on the red switch, stepped back, waiting for the sound of percolating coffee. Absently, she glanced into the adjacent living room, searching for Domino, the black stray with surprisingly symmetric white spots that she had adopted several years ago, when she had moved into the house. Her suspicion was that the cat had been abandoned by the previous owners, but her inquiries to this effect had been in vain. The cat presided over the household with exquisite grace and unquestioned authority.

"Domino, good morning!" Melanie smiled as she saw a black head pop up from the depths of the sofa and heard a questioning feline reply to her salutation. The cat jumped gracefully from the sofa, leaving a small, warm indentation on the mohair throw and in a moment was in her arms. Melanie stepped back into the kitchen and reached for the cat's food while Domino strained in her arms, anticipating breakfast.

Melanie had lived in this house in the heart of the historic district for several years before marrying Brian. When she had married, her new husband had the good sense to give up his bachelor pad near the western end of Tradd Street and move into his wife's home at the eastern end of the street, obviously a much-loved retreat from the world, tastefully decorated and within a half-block of the Battery and historic Church Street.

Ten minutes later, the cat outside and the newspaper indoors, Melanie sipped coffee and read the headlines. "Local Architect Found Dead" announced the front page. "Mark Caxton Fatally Stabbed in His Home." Melanie cocked her head, listening for sounds of Kate stirring upstairs. Hearing nothing, she read with interest.

Local architect Mark Caxton was found dead at his Lamont Street home early yesterday morning. His wife, ophthalmologist Dr. Katharine Porter Caxton, and her friend, Laura Lindross, reportedly found the body and summoned police by calling 911. Dr. Caxton was reportedly seeing patients at the time of her husband's murder. They had been married for more than two years. She is said to be staying at the house of a friend and could not be reached for comment.

Ms. Laura Lindross, a writer of mysteries, was at her King Street home last night. She stated that Mark Caxton was "clearly dead, although recently so," when Kate Caxton summoned her to survey the body. She noted no evidence of a struggle before taking her friend to another part of the house and calling police. Ms. Lindross has re-sided in Charleston for a month and describes herself as "saddened by this unexpected tragedy which is an unwelcome real-life reflection of my vocation as a mystery novelist."

Luke Grimke, a fellow architect who knew Caxton for more than ten years, was reached for comment at Kiawah Island, where he had spent the morning golfing until police informed him of the tragedy. "I can't assimilate a motive or a sustained belief that he is actually dead. We were friends for many years and had the greatest respect for one another." Grimke dismisses the suggestion that he and Caxton were dueling over a townhouse contract commissioning the construction of the much talked about Palmetto Pointe development. "You win some, you lose some. If Mark had gotten the contract, I would have wished him well. He's got an excellent eye, a unique sense of space and atmosphere; he would have done Charleston proud."

Charleston police have also questioned Amanda Michaels, an ex-girlfriend of Mark Caxton's, as part of their investigation. She co-owns Michaels & Moore Gallery on East Bay Street. Ms. Michaels did not respond to phone calls from The Post & Courier.

Police plan to question Mr. Caxton's business partner, Brian Chivas, who is currently out of the country on business. Caxton and Chivas grew up together locally, attending Porter-Gaud together in the 1970s. They were roommates at Yale University for four years and returned to Charleston in 1985, establishing Caxton, Chivas & Ross on Broad Street.

Georgiana Gisele "Gigi " Ross, who has already been questioned by police, joined the firm in 1998 from New York City. When contacted at her Wentworth Street home last night, Ms. Ross had this to say: "People like Mark are what makes the world go around. He was sweet, dedicated, and extremely good at what he did. I can't even begin to guess why someone wanted him dead. I'm stunned and saddened, and my thoughts are with his wife and family." Ms. Ross reports that Mr. Caxton appeared to be in good spirits on Friday night as they concluded a business meeting in their Broad Street offices. "He appeared untroubled, confident in our firm's ability to secure the Palmetto Pointe contract."

Mr. Caxton was autopsied late last night at Charleston Medical Center. The results of the autopsy are expected to be made public sometime tomorrow. The investigation remains open, with no suspects identified so far, according to police.

Mr. Caxton is survived by his wife, three sisters, and six nieces and nephews. Funeral services will be held at St. Philip's Church on Tuesday morning at 11:00.

Melanie sighed and put down the paper. She gazed out the windows leading into her walled, Italian-style garden. Domino was playing in the sunshine, and red hibiscus blossoms swayed in the breeze. She glanced at the clock that read 7:37. Perhaps, twenty-four hours ago, Mark had still been alive, without any suspicion of the brevity of the time he had left. She refilled her coffee mug and passed through the French doors into the garden. Settling into a cushioned lawn chaise, she allowed her robe to slip open, enjoying the warm sun on her naked skin, knowing that her small garden was sheltered from neighbors' eyes.

She and Brian had fun out here, she reflected, smiling as she thought of her husband's imminent return. Domino came and lay down next to her, tail swishing in the air, small pink nose wrinkling appreciatively, as the breeze danced across his fur. A fly buzzed around Melanie's head. She drifted, the stress of the last day catching up with her.

The click of a camera made her eyes pop open. She saw a tousled head above the wall and gave an exclamation of disgust. Reporters! Of course, how could she not have thought of that? The place would be crawling with them. She slipped back into the house, preceded by the cat, his fur rising along his back.

It was going to be a long day.

Upstairs, Kate lay wide awake and dry-eyed in the mahogany bed. She had slept very little. She had heard Melanie quietly go downstairs and was grateful for her thoughtful friend. For a moment, Kate considered telling Melanie everything, but discarded this notion almost immediately. She looked around the neatly-appointed guest room. Sun spilled into the east-facing window, and the pastel hue of the house next door looked back at her. For a moment her mood lightened. Charleston was beautiful. The historic district, with its Caribbean and European influences melding to create a perfect, romantic city, was unique in its feel and possibilities. Then sadness again suffused her as she thought of Mark and their early days together.

Her bedroom door creaked open, and Domino came into the room. Barely glancing at her, he made his way to the wide window, jumping up onto the sill in a flash of glossy fur. He licked his paws, then settled into a dense ball, suddenly a perfect sculpture. *There are no ordinary cats*, Kate remembered the famous quotation by Colette as she got out of bed and stopped to stroke the cat before disappearing into the adjacent bathroom.

When Kate walked into the kitchen fifteen minutes later, Melanie had already secreted the newspaper and was making fresh coffee. She came over to give her friend a close hug, then handed her a cup of coffee.

"Good morning, how're you doing?" Melanie was pleased that Kate had showered and didn't appear to be moping. "Did you sleep well?"

Kate shrugged. "I think I slept a little, the bed was really comfortable. Thank you so much for letting me stay, it helped me a lot." She took a sip of steaming coffee. It was black just as Melanie knew she liked it. "I think it's starting to sink in, you know, that he's gone."

Melanie looked at her soberly. "Yeah, he is," she agreed. "You stay here as long as you like, honey. It's difficult for all of us. I like your company too, you know. Mark would've wanted us to get through it together."

Kate looked out the window, listening to the church bells that one always heard throughout Charleston on Sunday morning. "Actually, I think it would be better for me to go to home," she said slowly. "I know it sounds odd, but I might even go into work for a bit, just to tie up some loose ends. I need to take my mind off things, and, God knows, there's always chaos at work. Even on a Sunday. That might actually be a good thing for me right now. I need to stop thinking so much." She gave her friend a weak smile. "It's a form of mental torture, you know. I see him everywhere, hear his voice, feel his touch." She put down her mug and wrapped slim arms around herself. Melanie noticed her wedding band glinting in the sun. "I can't ever have him back."

They sat in silence for a while, then spoke of the funeral plans that Kate had decided on yesterday after talking to Mark's oldest sister. "We want it to be a small funeral, but I know it won't be. He had too many friends, too many acquaintances. Most people knew who he was. I only hope the reporters and television crews won't be obnoxious."

"They already are." Melanie told her about the peeping Tom who had crawled into her neighbor's garden, and both women managed a weak smile. "I guess it is kind of funny when you think about it, there I am, half naked…"

Melanie went to the front door and identified several reporters and a TV van lying in wait. "I guess we'll just have to sneak out," she said.

The prospect of eluding the media was oddly appealing. Thirty minutes later, the women were dressed and considering the escape route. Finally, they decided Kate would slip out the back while Melanie distracted the reporters at the front door with a brief statement before heading to the gallery to join Amanda.

When she arrived at Michaels & Moore Gallery, Melanie was shocked at how tired Amanda looked. Her already lean body looked even thinner. Limp blonde hair hung down her back. Amanda's brown eyes were sad as she turned to greet her friend.

"Hi, Melanie," she said. "How'd things go yesterday?"

Melanie felt a stab of guilt for having left Amanda to run the gallery all by herself from noon until nine o'clock last night without even calling her to check in. And Amanda had come in and unlocked the place this morning, too.

Melanie sighed. She had been so wrapped up in providing emotional support for Kate, her other best friend.

"I think Kate's doing okay," she said. "I took her home with me late yesterday afternoon, we just talked, watched a movie. She's already talked with Mark's sisters, and they're getting funeral plans straightened out." She didn't mention that Kate was thinking of going to work. "You, on the other hand, don't look so hot." She eyed Amanda with concern.

"Me? I'm okay," Amanda returned unconvincingly. "I

confess I didn't sleep well at all, but it's not really Mark specifically. I mean, I did love him once, very much, it's just that it's a shock to find out how short life really is. It makes me want to tell everyone to just get along and be good to each other."

"I know, Mandy, you're right. It's like Vladimir Nabokov said: 'Life is just a brief crack of light between two vast eternities.' It's easy to forget that." Melanie looked around the gallery of which they were so proud and felt the memories pervading the space. She put her arm around her friend and checked her watch. "Come on, it's nearly eleven o'clock. Let's go get some lunch."

They walked up East Bay to Magnolia's. Already many patrons were present having brunch. The hostess surveyed the sunken dining room and led them down the steps to a table by the window. The dark wooden floor and snow-white tablecloths complemented the multiple prints on the walls, all different artists' renditions of the magnolia flower, the blossom that most nearly epitomizes the South. Although she could not see it from where she sat, Melanie was proud that one of her paintings hung at the far end of the room. A small print that Amanda had made hung in the second dining room, beyond the kitchen.

"Good morning." Their server, in black pants and white blouse, materialized promptly. "May I get you something to drink?"

Both women ordered unsweetened iced tea, then Amanda settled on the Wadmalaw baby greens; Melanie selected the spinach fettucine with salmon. They came to Magnolia's often enough to know exactly what they wanted. For a while, neither woman spoke.

"So, Mandy, did you still love him?" Melanie finally asked.

Amanda smoothed her hair from her face. She spoke softly. "Not only did I still love him, but I think I was still in love with him," she said. "I know that now, although it's a little too late." She put down her fork. "I really thought he was the one. Hell, I think he thought he was the one. You know, the first time we made love, he looked at me afterwards and said, 'Did you think you'd ever find me?'" She smiled as she remembered. "That was Mark, so sweetly self-centered that you never realized it was all about him until it was too late." She frowned. "I couldn't believe it when he left me for Kate. Then I met her and saw how perfect she was for him. It's funny, I never blamed her for how things turned out. I blamed him."

Melanie spoke abruptly. "Mandy, why were you late to the gallery yesterday morning? It's not like you to be late." Amanda was one of those people who was always reliable.

Amanda didn't answer immediately. "I overslept," she finally said. "I know, I never do that, but it's true." She looked at Melanie. "I'd like it if you believed me."

"Of course I believe you." Melanie heard the words come out of her mouth, but knew they weren't true. If Amanda had overslept, she would have said so when she got to the gallery. She would have apologized profusely. As Melanie remembered, Amanda had come in from the back, lingering in the storage room until Melanie called out to her, hoping perhaps that Melanie would think she'd been back there for a while, making coffee and glancing through the paper. They opened the gallery at seven-thirty on Saturday from April until the first of October to take advantage of the early morning foot traffic of the tourist season. Amanda had been at least twenty minutes late. Melanie had seen her hurrying down the alleyway from State Street at ten minutes of eight.

Amanda's voice was so low, Melanie barely heard her. "Did you say anything to the police? About me being late?" Her hair obscured her face as she hung her head.

Melanie reached over and made eye contact with her friend. "Honey, you have nothing to be worried about. Of course I believe you. And as far as I'm concerned, we got to the gallery together, both of us just in time to open at seven thirty."

Amanda looked at her friend and smiled. "Great, Melanie, thanks."

Her friend smiled back. "No problem," she said thoughtfully. "Remember, it's my alibi too."

7

Cleo Cooper let out a shriek.

"Hey, that's my boss!" She squealed to no one in particular. "Omigod, Mr. Caxton's been killed!" She stopped teasing her bleach-blonde hair and stared at the television set. A bubblegum-colored towel covered her from chest to mid-thigh. Her toenails were newly pink.

A dissolute-appearing young man wearing faded swim trunks and holding a joint in one hand came into the living room from the bedroom where he had been listening to music while Cleo got ready for a night on the town. It always took her hours to get ready, and now here she was, shrieking about something already, and it wasn't even dark yet. "What the hell's goin' on?" He asked with a modicum of interest, taking a drag of weed.

She didn't take her eyes off Live Five news, where Mark Caxton's death was the lead story. "You know that architectural firm I started working for a couple months ago? Looks like one of 'em got stabbed to death yesterday." She sat down on the peppermint-striped sofa, mesmerized. "Oh God, Joey, ain't it awful?"

Joey sat down next to her and watched an interview with Melanie Moore Chivas, who was described as a friend of the widow and wife of the deceased's business partner, taped as she left the house for work that morning. "...and I devoutly hope and pray, as we all do, that whoever did this will be brought swiftly to justice." Reporters called out questions as Melanie put on her sunglasses and disappeared down Tradd Street to the gallery. The commentator's face appeared on the screen, along with the Channel Five logo. "We'll keep you up to date on this puzzling and heartbreaking story as the details continue to unfold."

Cleo turned to Joey and shivered. "Wow, that's weird. I wonder what happened? I just saw him Friday afternoon. He was a really nice guy, actually, let me go home a little early that day. Remember, we went to the beach so you could surf a little more?"

"Yeah, I remember," Joey looked thoughtful. "Something must be going on. Rich guy, lotta enemies, I'm not sure I like you workin' there, sugar."

Cleo snuggled up against him, eyes bright. "Hey, you s'pose the police will wanna question me? I was one of the last people to see him alive, I bet! Maybe I know something that I don't know I know. I should start thinking about it."

Joey pulled her towel free and shed his swim trunks in the process. He pulled her toward the bedroom. "Here, I'll give you somethin' to think about." Cleo giggled and then laughed as he tickled her rib cage, her momentary uneasiness forgotten.

* * * * *

Luke stood in front of the bathroom mirror and carefully fastened his tie.

He was looking forward to his business dinner at the Peninsula Room. For several years now, he had been considering a partner and believed he had finally found the right person. Luke had chosen a dark charcoal suit with white shirt and pale silver tie. His reflection gazed back at him, the blue eyes thoughtful. The ornate mirror was placed above a large sink made of polished granite. The large sunken bathtub to his left was constructed of the same expensive material.

He noted with pleasure that Veronica's silver-blonde hair contrasted nicely with the tub surrounding her. Pink tulips in a silver vase accented the iridescent bubbles that lay heaped on her chest as she read a magazine, her little tortoiseshell reading glasses perched demurely on the end of her nose. She reached out languid fingers for a champagne flute on the adjacent marble floor and caught him watching her. She smiled, and her nose wrinkled with pleasure. He walked over, hands still on the Windsor knot, and bestowed a kiss on her pale pink lips.

Many people were surprised to learn that Luke was dating a woman his own age. He did not understand why. Veronica was smart and funny. She was warm, adventuresome, and had a glorious sense of self. She kept her hair pulled back in a restrained knot at the back of her head, but, when the time was right, she certainly knew how to let her hair down, too. In every sense of the word. She was, to him, the personification of elegance. Unconsciously his words echoed his thoughts.

"See you later, beautiful," he murmured as her warm, wet fingers caressed his cheek. "Have a relaxing evening."

Veronica spent most nights at his place on Legare Street, though, if she did not, she never offered an explanation. Ironically, this did not bother him. He reflected that perhaps he enjoyed the mystery of her. *Maybe*, he thought, *I'm not the only guy she's seeing*. This bothered him a bit, but also appealed to his sense of competition. He was sure he would win her over completely in time.

"Good night, darling," she replied. "I hope the meeting goes as well as you hope it will." Luke left her ensconced amidst the bubbles, rose-scented steam rising from her damp skin.

Luke bypassed the elevator to walk down the four flights

of mahogany staircase that ended in his impressive entryway. It was made of old Italian marble, each piece meticulously cut in Italy over two hundred years ago, packed and transported across the Atlantic Ocean specifically for what was to become his house. He rested a well-groomed hand on the elaborate newel post and surveyed his domain.

He had recently bought and renovated this imposing four-story home, which had been on the market for a year with a million dollar price tag. Wallpaper dating back to World War I had decorated the walls of the long-empty home before he had embarked on his renovation. The drawers of a built-in cabinet in one of the six huge bedrooms were still lined with faded yellow newspaper from a Sunday edition dated June 23, 1935.

Luke's renovations had been dramatic and extensive. The kitchen and four baths had been completely re-done, as new plumbing and electricity was placed. Each splendid room was painted, and the original wooden floors were exposed and polished. Moldings were restored. The bedrooms on the second floor became guest quarters, while the rooms on the third and fourth floors were enlarged and modernized to include master bedroom, adjacent bath with sunken tub that Veronica loved, sun room, and study. A rooftop solarium and terraced garden afforded a wrap-around view of the peninsula and Atlantic Ocean.

Luke walked through the entryway, which was illuminated by a crystal chandelier, a larger version of which decorated the formal dining room to his left, and opened the massive oak door. He always enjoyed this view of his picturesque street and the subsequent descent down the steep, stately steps. He got into his Jaguar and drove to the restaurant where he had it valet-parked.

Stepping into the bright lobby of the new restaurant, Luke spotted his guest almost immediately. *A punctual person*, he thought. *We're off to a good start.*

* * * * *

Kate sighed as she turned off her Dictaphone and put the last chart on the pile. She saw it was nearly eight o'clock. Much as she enjoyed her work as a surgeon, the stress and constant worry was having its effect. Her ulcer from medical school was coming back, and her body was keenly aware of her lack of sleep from the night before. She jumped as a voice spoke from the doorway.

"Sorry to bother you, Dr. Caxton." It was one of her third-year residents, Dr. Will Fennell, craning his head timidly around the door frame. "We've got a patient downstairs; we were wondering if you could take a look at him. Looks like a traction retinal detachment involving the macular center."

Kate slipped on her white coat and made her way down the hall with the resident. "Tell me what's going on."

Her resident prattled on obediently as they entered the elevator for the first-floor clinic. "Forty-eight year old African-American male, eleven year history of diabetes, had PRP about three years ago elsewhere. Thinks both eyes were done. Nothing since then. Blood sugar poorly controlled, averaging 250 to 300. Two-year history of painless progressive loss of vision, says things got really bad last week sometime. Came in through the ER today. Left eye is basically toast, looks like combined traction and rhegmatogenous detachment, chronic. Right eye is the one I wanted you to look at."

Kate sighed. Probably the patient had been relying on

just one eye for a while. People were often unaware of progressive damage in one eye because the fellow eye afforded good vision. Then, when vision loss occurred in the second eye, emergency visits to her office occurred. Unfortunately, that raised the stakes even higher when considering treatment options and management. "Any vitreous hemorrhage?" She wondered aloud.

"Not yet."

Surveying her patient's severe proliferative diabetic retinopathy through the slit lamp with a ninety diopter lens and again with the indirect ophthalmoscope, Kate was inclined to agree with her resident. The first eye was inoperable, with a thinned retina and multiple posterior holes. The second eye would need vitrectomy, membrane peeling, and supplemental panretinal photocoagulation with the endolaser as soon as possible. She explained the risks, benefits, and alternatives to surgery and left her resident to finalize things. They would add the patient to her Wednesday operating room schedule.

Kate was still mulling over the surgical plan and the patient's unfortunate situation when she got to her office. Shedding her white coat, she collected her briefcase and caught a glimpse of herself in the narrow mirror on the wall next to her desk. Her face was pale, and her eyes looked bleak, matching her short-sleeved gray turtleneck and skirt. She had pulled her reddish hair back from her face today; this made her look stern. And sad, she realized. *No wonder my resident didn't want to bother me*, she thought; *I look ready to bite someone's head off.*

As if on cue, the resident reappeared. "I just wanted to say how sorry I am, Dr. Caxton, about your husband. Let me know if there's anything I can do."

"Thank you, I appreciate it, Will," Kate responded. "I'm

okay for now, just sometimes it feels good to get lost in all the work that piles up around here." Her resident returned her wan smile and left.

Kate left shortly thereafter. She was looking forward to the walk home.

* * * * *

Melanie swore under her breath. She was running late. It was already after eight o'clock, and, again, she'd left Amanda to close the gallery. She had hoped to be able to swing by the grocery store before she fetched Brian at the airport—he liked a well-stocked refrigerator as much as the next guy—but now she would not have time. She would collect him, and they could shop together on the way home. She always enjoyed that.

Melanie let herself into the house and was met by Domino, mewing piteously as if he had not been fed for a week. She went to the refrigerator and stopped short, remembering there was neither tuna nor the dry cat food that her veterinarian persisted in recommending as an integral part of a balanced feline diet. *Another thing to get at the Harris Teeter; I should really make a list.* Melanie quickly fed the cat some turkey left over from sandwiches she had made on Friday. "Now, don't tell your Daddy we did that," she admonished. Brian was particular about keeping people food away from the cat. She smiled indulgently, watching Domino, then grabbed the car keys and hurried out the front door.

8

"Ladies and gentlemen, this is your pilot speaking. We are beginning our initial descent into the Charleston area. It is a pleasant evening, with seventy-two degrees and clear skies. We should be arriving at the terminal in approximately twenty minutes."

Even without the pilot's announcement, Brian's subconscious had registered an adjustment in the monotonous thrum of the jet's engines; he slowly surfaced from the dark landscape of semi-sleep where Mark's death was tormenting and confusing him. He flexed his fingers and experimentally stretched, extending his legs into the aisle before reluctantly opening his eyes. The flight attendant, who had been keeping a solicitous eye on her handsome, but restless, passenger, noticed him emerging from his uneasy sleep and handed him a small towel, neatly rolled, steamed and scented with lemon. She received a sheepish smile in return.

Brian turned and looked out the window of the first-class cabin. The towel was warm in his hands, but his insides felt cold as he saw the tiny twinkling lights of the Charleston environs in the twilight below. He could not grasp the concept of Mark's death and was not looking forward to stepping into the reality that awaited in Charleston. Melanie had already told him that the police were expecting him to come to the police station very early tomorrow morning for questioning.

He brightened at the thought of seeing Melanie and began to assemble his belongings. His portable computer was in his briefcase. He stuffed his copies of *Sports Illustrated* and *GQ*, hastily grabbed during his layover at

Atlanta's Hartsfield International Airport, in the seat pocket in front of him. Perhaps the next guy having to fly the friendly skies would be grateful for the diversion.

Ten minutes later, the aircraft landed with a small bump and was maneuvered to the appropriate gate. Brian stood, briefcase in hand, and was the second person to emerge from the jetway. He looked around for his wife and spotted her almost immediately.

"Hi, honey!" She was in his arms. He kissed her hair, then her lips, and thought again how lucky he was to have found her. She gazed at him with shining eyes. "I missed you so much!"

"I missed you too, sweetie." He took her hand. As they walked, they began to talk about the recent tragedy. "Sorry to bring up a bad subject, but how's everything going with the investigation?"

Melanie brought him up to date as they came to the baggage claim. As always, Brian traveled light; they were awaiting just one black leather suitcase.

"There it is." Melanie spotted it before he did. He hoisted it free of the surrounding duffle bags and other luggage. Then they made their way into the warm southern night. Palmetto trees and hibiscus decorated the stairs leading down to the parking lot. The sulfur-sweetened air welcomed him. Brian was impressed that Melanie had succeeded in parking their SUV in fairly close proximity to the walkway, but, then again, he reflected, it was a fairly small airport; parking was usually not too difficult to find.

"How's Domino?" he asked as he settled, by silent understanding, into the driver's seat.

Melanie fastened her seat belt and smiled. "He's fine," she responded, then frowned. "But we do have to stop at the Harris Teeter on the way home, we're out of some things, including his tuna."

Brian fiddled with the radio station. "Okay, no problem," he agreed, "I bet we need beer, too."

He stopped at the exit gate to pay the cashier, then got on the curving boulevard that led from the airport to I-26. Despite the open road, Melanie reflected, her husband was true to form as he caught sight of a slow driver in the left lane. Brian loved rhapsodizing about the efficiencies of the European road, specifically the German discipline behind the wheel. He gestured with disdain. "Would you look at that. The guy's rolling along on his spare, talking on his cell phone. American drivers...unbelievable."

Melanie hid a smile.

"How's Kate taking it?" her husband wondered next.

Melanie wrinkled her forehead. "You know, either she's taking it really well, or she's in complete denial." She turned to her husband. "She went to work today!"

Brian raised his eyebrows. "Poor thing. Sounds like it hasn't hit home yet. We're really gonna have to be there for her when it does."

Melanie nodded, and they were silent, both thinking of the tragedy that had occurred.

"Tell me more about the actual murder." The request sounded unreal to Brian's ears as he said it, but he needed to hear everything Melanie knew.

As they approached the end of the highway, Brian got into the left lane and took the Meeting Street exit. There were multiple stoplights in this somewhat rough part of town, but as they drove past the visitors' center, the beauty of the historic section slowly became apparent. Beyond Calhoun Street, once considered the dividing line between safe and unsafe neighborhoods, the Ansonborough homes became stately.

A left turn onto Broad Street took them past the dark

windows of Caxton, Chivas & Ross. A small group of tourists listened to their tour guide under a golden street light, probably enjoying the ever-popular Ghost Tour. Melanie remembered going on it herself once or twice.

"Honey, don't forget, the grocery store," she reminded her husband, as he got into the right-hand lane for the turn onto East Bay Street.

"Oh yeah, I forgot." Brian turned left instead; they traveled up East Bay, past the Michaels & Moore gallery, past the old Market, once used to sell slaves, and to the corner of Hasell Street. Soon this would be Palmetto Pointe territory. Brian took the turn into Harris Teeter and parked the SUV in a corner of the lot. Just as raindrops started to fall, they scurried up the wooden steps of the low-slung, warehouse-like building.

* * * * *

Luke noticed raindrops pelting the window as he ordered coffee. The Peninsula Room had a limited number of tables overlooking the courtyard. Lush with palmetto trees, hibiscus, and other tropical foliage around a sunken goldfish pool, the view was coveted. After nightfall, golden footlights illuminated greenery alive with the sound of cicadas. Luke knew the air would be warm and moist. The mystery of the South was palpable and carefully cultivated at most downtown restaurants.

"Just black is fine," Luke instructed their obsequious server. He had never gotten on the espresso/latte/cappuccino bandwagon. Coffee was coffee. He preferred it black. He was pleased when his guest ordered the same as he did. *Great minds think alike.*

It had been an illuminating meal. Luke was pleased with

the other architect. He would offer the job at the end of the week. But first there was some other business to take care of. He had to make sure that he could afford to take on an expensive new colleague.

Luke paid the bill. Ten minutes later he was in his car, but not ready to go home quite yet. One of Charleston's many church bells had just sounded the nine o'clock hour as he turned onto East Bay Street.

* * * * *

Inside the Harris Teeter grocery store, Brian wrestled a shopping cart free while Melanie was distracted by the flowers displayed near the fresh produce. She selected a dozen purple irises with associated greenery and had them wrapped. Catching up with her husband, she dropped the irises in the cart, next to fresh tomatoes and Vidalia onions.

"I thought I'd make some omelets for breakfast tomorrow," Brian explained as he added fresh spinach to the other produce.

"Mmm, sounds perfect," Melanie smiled as she thought of the occasional lazy weekday morning they spent together, where they both ended up being late to work and not caring. Then she remembered that Brian was due at the police station at seven o'clock, bright and early.

"What do you think the police will ask you?" she said as they selected yogurt, eggs, and cheddar cheese.

"Probably just various questions about Mark," Brian shook his head. "I knew him better than anyone. And I sure as hell can't think of a reason for someone to kill him."

"Do you have any ideas at all?" Melanie persisted. "I mean, what could the motives be? Greed? Jealousy? Betrayal? Sex?"

"All those, I guess." Brian was thoughtful. "He had money, but who would kill him for that? His wife? Me or Gigi, his business partners?" He paused. "As for jealousy, I can't think of anyone, except maybe Luke? But he seems centered and sane, if a bit egocentric. Plus he apparently has an alibi."

"Yeah, golfing on Kiawah is what Amanda told me," Melanie interrupted. "That leaves betrayal. And sex. Would he have told you if the marriage was in trouble? I just can't imagine either of them cheating," she mused. "So, girlfriend or jealous lover is probably not high on the list of possible scenarios."

Brian seemed about to answer when they rounded the corner into the frozen food aisle and nearly bumped into Amanda, who gave a squeal of delight.

"Brian, welcome back!"

"Mandy, how are you doing?" Brian enveloped her in a bear hug, noticing her unaccustomed pallor and red-rimmed eyes. He could feel her bony rib cage as he hugged her.

Amanda gave him a big smile and a quick kiss. "How was Paris? Did you stave off all those seductive suggestions from the sexy French mademoiselles?" She winked at Melanie, still grinning, while Brian grimaced and rolled his eyes heavenward. Amanda continued to tease her friend. "I know, you suffer because you're beautiful."

The banter continued for a minute more, until the conversation inevitably turned to Mark. Amanda's eyes filled with tears.

"Do you have any idea what might have led to this? You knew him so well." She watched Brian hopefully.

As Brian slowly shook his head, Melanie explained, "Maybe the police will be able to draw some information out of him that he doesn't know he knows. He's going for his interview early tomorrow morning."

"Oh, well, don't let me keep you," Amanda offered. "You probably want to get home and rest a little before you have to head down there tomorrow."

"We should probably get going," Brian admitted. "Take care of yourself, Mandy," he added, once again taking in her disheveled appearance.

Leaving Amanda to finish her shopping, Melanie and Brian made their way to the check-out line. The lines were short, and, as they tried to leave the store, it became clear why. Torrential rain engulfed them as they exited through the sliding doors. Melanie had never known it to rain anywhere the way it rained in the South.

"Make a break for it," Brian advised, and they ducked through the dark parking lot toward the car, which was impossible to visualize through sheets of heavy rain.

Brian had just started loading groceries into the back of the SUV when Melanie gave a quick exclamation of disgust. "Oh, rats, I forgot the tuna for Domino! I have to go back."

"I'll pull the car up front for when you're done," Brian said, pulling the grocery cart closer to the car.

"Okay, honey, thanks." Melanie gave his cheek a quick kiss and tasted rainwater on her lips. He glanced at her affectionately, sluicing water from his hair before reaching for more grocery bags. "Hurry back, honey," he smiled.

As she raced back through the rain toward the golden door of the Harris Teeter, she thought she heard more words, whipped quickly away in the windy night. "I love you, Mrs. Chivas."

After Melanie paid for her dozen cans of tuna in water—early on, the cat had demonstrated a taste for superior food—she hurried toward the door. She did not see Brian waiting in the special traffic lane immediately out front, which was separated from the rest of the parking lot by a central island landscaped in shrubbery.

With a puzzled expression marring her delicate features, she glanced around the parking lot, but in the rain visibility was poor. It occurred to her that Brian could have taken an extra turn around the store so as not to block traffic while waiting for her.

After a few minutes, Melanie moved into the downpour toward the spot where they had parked earlier. As she came upon the car, she noticed the tail lights were on and hurried toward the passenger door, which was closer to her. *He could have gotten sidetracked by the news of Mark's death on the radio.* Her door was locked. Brian's door seemed to be open, but he was not in the car. Now thoroughly drenched, Melanie went around the back of the car. His door was partially open, but her husband was nowhere in sight. She advanced and was trying to see beyond the half-open door when her foot hit something heavy and soft. Looking down through the darkness, the first thing Melanie noticed was irises, dimly illuminated by the light from the dashboard. She kneeled down, reaching toward the scattered flowers and the dark shape sprawled at her feet.

She heard a woman screaming and realized it was herself.

9

Afterward, Melanie could never remember exactly what happened. People had come. She remembered Amanda's pale face. She sat on the wet cement, cradling her husband's head, aware of the lingering warmth of his skin against her icy fingers. It was important to keep him warm. She pressed more and more closely against his body. An ambulance came, red lights throbbing grotesquely in the storm-streaked night, siren shrieking. When they pulled her away from Brian, rain was mixed indiscriminately with the tears on her face and the dark sticky blood on her hands.

A paramedic wrapped her in a blanket. Then she was helped into a squad car. They drove her to the hospital; a sympathetic doctor examined her. They washed her hands and her face, which were covered in blood. Images floated in front of her, and she was incapable of speech. Someone brought coffee, which she clutched but could not drink. She was shaking, shivering uncontrollably. A resident sat with her and explained gently that she was in shock. Other emergency room patients came in and were sent to x-ray or rushed to the operating room.

Finally, someone came and told her Brian was dead. She was surprised that they thought she had not known. They said that he had been stabbed, his aorta transected. They said he had not suffered.

Gentle hands brought more coffee and another blanket. She was told that the police needed to speak with her. She was aware of two officers who were ushered into the small cubicle. Their mouths moved, but she heard no words. She became aware of a loud rushing noise in her ears and wondered about that.

When she finally fainted, no one was very surprised.

* * * * *

"Godammit," Detective Jeff Marcus swore into the handpiece of the telephone outside the main doors of the emergency room at Charleston Medical Center. "Who's the fucking genius who decided we should question Chivas the day after he came back into town? It's obvious the guy knew something!"

He ran his hand distractedly through his hair. "No, I don't know whether his wife knows anything. Poor thing just passed out cold when we tried to talk to her—turned white as a sheet and damn near hit the floor. Now she's sedated under twenty-three hour observation; they're not letting anyone near her."

He listened to the voice on the other end of the line. "Hell, yeah, we've got two guards posted with strict orders not to let anyone in...yeah, you do that, yeah, okay."

He slammed the phone into place and rubbed his eyes. It was going to be a long night.

He found Hobbs; they were about to leave for the station when a smartly dressed woman approached them. She wore a navy suit with a red pinstripe running through it and gave them a winsome smile.

They knew she was a reporter before she even opened her mouth.

"No comment," Hobbs got the words out before Marcus could. They left her standing in the lobby, mouth half-open like a fish gasping for air. Forewarned, they exited the hospital, where additional reporters, including the anchor from Channel Five, had already assembled.

"Officer, can you verify that the murdered man is Brian

Chivas, business associate of Mark Caxton?"

"Detective, rumor has it that this second death is closely linked with the death of Mark Caxton, the architect, yesterday morning."

"Officers, is it true that the victim was fatally stabbed?"

Hobbs and Marcus, tight-lipped, made it to their illegally parked squad car and drove away.

* * * * *

Amanda didn't know what to do. She had not even had the chance to talk to Melanie, or offer to go with her to the hospital, before the police had whisked her friend away.

She had seen a knot of people clustered around a car in the southeastern corner of the parking lot, an odd thing to do in the driving rain. Then a woman had screamed. Amanda saw a man speaking hurriedly into his cellular phone. As Amanda drew closer, nausea overcame her. Paralyzed with fear, she hung back for the few precious minutes before the police arrived. Melanie was taken away. And then a dark limp shape was loaded into the ambulance.

Pulling herself together, Amanda had found her car and followed at a safe distance to Charleston Medical Center. She had attempted to see Melanie twice, but was refused access to the ER both times.

Sitting in her car next to the ER entrance, Amanda saw Detective Marcus and his partner come out of the sliding doors of the ER. Grimly, they made it past reporters and TV cameras and sped away. Amanda wondered where they were going. *Perhaps to interview possible suspects.*

A sudden chill ran through her. Maybe they were going to interview her. And she wouldn't be at home because she had been at the scene of the crime.

Dully, Amanda started the car and left the hospital. She turned onto Calhoun Street and followed it to East Bay. She turned right and soon was passing the Harris Teeter on her left. Its parking lot was lit with large strobe lights and already cordoned off with yellow crime scene tape. The unrelenting words "Police Line Do Not Cross" were visible in the harsh glare of the artificial light.

For the first time, Amanda noticed the rain had stopped.

Brian must be dead, she thought, and emptiness filled her, followed by fear. She continued toward the Battery, her heart pounding like a jackhammer. Turning right onto Cumberland Street and making the next left onto State Street, she immediately saw the police car parked in front of her house. There was nothing for her to do but invite them in.

Amanda's house, a pink, two-storied gem, wider than it was deep, was tucked away from the street. Entering the front door, living room and drawing room were arranged on either side of the staircase, with a small kitchen on the north end of the first floor. Upstairs, the floor plan was the same, with study and bedroom next to the bath that overlay the kitchen.

Detective Marcus' dark hair and olive complexion made him look at home in Amanda's living room, which was simply furnished in a British Colonial style. Dark wood and built-in bookshelves on every wall along with hand-carved elephant figurines, silver vases, and classic leather furniture melded into a small but impressive living room. There were no windows on the back wall of the house, as its east side formed the west wall of an adjacent home. The general effect spoke of cozy solitude and happiness.

Amanda did not look happy as she answered yet another question. She looked scared. "I didn't see anyone I know besides Brian and Melanie. It looked as if they were just at the Harris Teeter to pick up a few things. I didn't see them in the check-out line, nor did I see them leaving the store."

Hobbs and Marcus exchanged glances before Hobbs continued. "So, even though, by your own admission, you have eaten nothing for two days, and it was pouring rain tonight, you went out to get groceries at about nine o'clock." Amanda opened her mouth, but Hobbs held up an admonishing forefinger. "Even after spending two exhausting days dealing with the brutal murder of your ex-lover, and, again by your own admission, not sleeping last night, you still summoned the energy to leave the house and shop. Accidentally, then, you say, you ran into two of your close acquaintances, only to discover minutes later that one of them had been murdered while you happened to be yards away."

A spark of anger lit up Amanda's eyes. "Until this very moment, I had no idea he was actually dead, Detective. Thank you for breaking the news to me in such a solicitous manner."

Marcus avoided Amanda's gaze until Hobbs spoke again. "We're just trying to solve two particularly heinous crimes, Ms. Michaels, and we're not big fans of coincidence. Please don't take it personally."

Amanda watched as the detectives got up and made their way to the front door. As Marcus shook her hand, she thought she detected sympathy and felt a little bit better.

As the police officers walked to the squad car, Marcus commented: "She's a tough lady, doesn't give away more than she has to, that's for sure."

Hobbs' impression was slightly different. "I think she's hiding something."

They drove down State Street and turned toward East

Bay, heading for Lamont. It was nearly ten o'clock, but all the lights in the Caxton residence were on.

Hobbs and Marcus approached the front door and rang the bell. Kate materialized behind the plate glass and did not seem surprised to see them. She was wearing surgical scrubs under a black turtleneck sweater, and her feet were bare. Her face looked pale, her red hair hanging limply around her face.

"Come in, gentlemen," she said. "How can I help you?" She held the door wide, but did not meet their eyes.

The two men settled into the airy living room and refused tea and coffee. As they told her of Brian's death, her face turned paler. Tears threatened, but her primary concern appeared to be her friend, now a widow as well. "May I go see her?"

Hobbs explained that Melanie was to have no visitors until the morning. Kate sat silently on the sofa, looking down at her hands. Hobbs noticed her long, thin fingers, more muscular than tapered, with the fingernails trimmed very short. The hands of a surgeon.

"May we ask your whereabouts earlier this evening?"

Kate spoke in a voice that was so quiet they had to strain to hear her. "I went up to work around six o'clock and finished there a couple hours later. I was home again after about nine o'clock." She explained that she had spoken with Laura shortly after arriving at home, but had no other alibis. "One of my residents saw me at work around eight o'clock," she offered. Hobbs thought her face was slightly tinged with green.

After Hobbs and Marcus took their leave, Kate went upstairs and vomited.

* * * * *

Their next stop was Luke Grimke's Legare Street home. The two detectives, who had heard as much as anyone about the architect's new digs, were disappointed when there was no answer to their repeated knocks with the lion-headed door knocker. Its reverberations were hard to miss. They surveyed the southern end of Legare, including the single slot for off-street parking tucked behind the wall that separated Grimke's corner house from the narrow sidewalk. It was empty; Luke's Jaguar was nowhere in sight.

Hobbs called in a report to police headquarters and decided on their next stop.

"Let's check up on that mystery novelist, Lindross. She was there for the first body; who knows what she can tell us regarding the second."

* * * * *

Security at Fort Sumter House was tight. As Marcus followed the security guard through the two sets of locked doors into a spacious lobby, he thought he knew why. The antique furniture and bold paintings on the ground floor alone appeared to be worth thousands of dollars. The floor leading to the double elevators was genuine Italian marble.

The guard called Laura's apartment from a sleek cell phone the size of a credit card. After receiving a favorable response, he accompanied them into the mirrored elevator and up to the eighth floor. A brisk rap on Laura's brightly painted door announced their arrival. She answered promptly.

Marcus surveyed the tall woman in front of him. She was wearing a heather-gray turtleneck and faded jeans. Her dark hair was pulled carelessly into a ponytail; her face was innocent of make-up. She held a cup of black coffee in one hand and gestured them into the apartment with the other, her eyes bright.

"Come in," she said. "Can I get you coffee, or maybe something else to drink?"

Hobbs declined for both of them and surveyed the small living room with interest. It was the big French windows with a sweeping view of the city's rooftops and Ashley River that took his breath away. Laura followed his gaze and smiled.

"Come on out on the balcony and take a look," she invited. "The view is the reason I bought this tiny place." They settled onto modern aluminum chairs that not only pleased the eye, reflecting the gray sheen of the water, but were extremely comfortable.

Marcus spoke first. "Nice view you've got here," he commented, somewhat unoriginally. Through the window, he noted Laura's computer glowing in the far end of the kitchen space. *She must like to look at the water while she writes.*

Laura smiled and took a sip of coffee, her eyes on his face. "Thank you very much, Detective. May I ask what brings you over to see me?" It seemed to Hobbs that her face was suddenly watchful, as if for bad news.

Hobbs turned in his chair and sighed. "I'm afraid we do have some more bad news, Ms. Lindross. Someone stabbed Brian Chivas in the chest earlier this evening. He was pronounced dead at CMC less than an hour ago. Roughly speaking, it appears that he and his partner, Mr. Caxton, were murdered in the same manner." He held up his hands, palm out, in a gesture of defeat. "It's looking like the two deaths are linked, and we're here to ask a couple of questions."

Laura's mouth opened, but she didn't say a word. Finally, she nodded. "That's fine," she managed. "I was up late anyway, writing, so it's not a problem."

Marcus glanced at his notebook. "Where were you tonight between nine and ten o'clock?"

"I was here, writing. You can verify that with Henry, our security guard. He saw me come in at about six o'clock."

Marcus nodded. "Did you see Kate Caxton today, or speak with her on the phone?"

Laura nodded slowly. "Yes, I spoke with her twice, first in the late morning. She had just come home from spending the night at Melanie Chivas' house. I called her around eleven o'clock. She seemed sad and said she was packing up Mark's things and might move out of the house if it continued to make her feel so bad."

Hobbs raised his eyebrows, but said nothing.

"Then I spoke with her about two hours ago. She had just returned from the hospital and was having difficulty getting to sleep. We talked about getting away from Charleston next weekend, maybe going to one of the spas on Hilton Head or something. Then she said she was tired and was going to try to sleep because she has a full clinic schedule tomorrow."

Hobbs nodded. It dovetailed completely with Kate's account. "Did you have any contact with Melanie Chivas or Amanda Michaels today?"

"No," Laura shook her head. "They're not really my friends, Kate is."

Finally the detectives got up to take their leave. Idly, Marcus said: "What's your new novel about?"

Laura smiled faintly. "I think my writer's block is gone. You might not be surprised to learn it's a murder mystery that takes place in Charleston."

* * * * *

Their last stop that night was Gigi Ross's elegant brick home on Wentworth Street.

"She's just down the street from the Harris Teeter, can't be more than a couple hundred yards," Hobbs observed. They looked down toward East Bay, where the crime scene was just out of their view.

There was no answer to the doorbell. The two police officers were just returning to their squad car when a woman, walking her dog up the sidewalk of the next house, stopped them. The dog was a tiny dachshund with liquid brown eyes and a mincing gait.

"If you're looking for Ms. Ross, I think she took Max for a run on the beach. I saw her load him into the car around nine o'clock." The woman looked around, as if expecting headlights at any minute. "She should be home soon."

Marcus thanked her, took her name and address, then joined his partner in the car. It was nearly eleven o'clock. He called in a report, and they drove to the police station. Gigi would be questioned in the morning.

10

It was not yet light when Gigi's alarm clock went off. It was six o'clock. She had been awake anyway, Max's big body lying warm across her legs.

She sighed. Max raised his head, hoping it was time for his morning walk. He had thoroughly enjoyed the couple of hours on Folly Beach the night before, Gigi reflected.

She got up and put on leggings and her black hooded sweatshirt. The dog's toenails clicked on the polished floor and then were silent as he traversed Persian throw rugs on the way to the front door. Gigi did not lock the front door as they left the house. It was early, Ansonborough was safe, and she had the dog to protect her.

They would not be gone long.

They walked west on Wentworth, then followed Meeting Street down the peninsula to White Point Gardens. Max's Kuvasz features, outlined by his snowy fur, seemed to be smiling as he pranced along the Battery. The sun came up in a mass of peachy gold and pink clouds. Gigi could feel her spirits lift as she watched the sunrise. She walked around the curve onto East Battery, leaving the sight of James Island for a bird's eye view of historic Fort Sumter with the Atlantic Ocean beyond. Gigi continued up East Bay, passing the massive homes frequently featured on the Travel Channel and then the equally well-known Rainbow Row on her left. The pastel exteriors looked fresh and clean in the early morning sunlight.

Arriving home around seven o'clock, Gigi found the two detectives waiting for her.

"Good morning, gentlemen. Please, come in," she greeted them as she entered the house. "Is there something I can help you with today?"

Marcus broke the news. "Ms. Ross, we need to know where you were between nine and ten o'clock last night. There has been another murder. Brian Chivas was stabbed to death outside the Harris Teeter last night."

"You've got to be joking," Gigi's hand flew to her chest. "Just down the street from here? Is this related to Mark's death? Is it the same person?" She sat down in the nearest chair.

"We don't know that yet, Ms. Ross," Hobbs continued, "that's why we need your help. Can you tell us where you were last night? We came by to ask you some questions, but your neighbor said you had left at around nine o'clock."

"I took Max for a run on Folly Beach last night," Gigi nodded. "I think we must have left here at about nine; we were back well before midnight."

Marcus and Hobbs exchanged glances. Her story checked out with what the neighbor had told them.

"Is there anyone who could place you at Folly Beach last night?" Marcus wondered.

"I wasn't there with anyone, just Max," Gigi answered. "There were other people on the beach, though; I'm sure they would remember me as the woman with the big white dog," she added, glancing down at Max lying at her feet. "But I don't know their names, I don't know how you would contact them."

Marcus and Hobbs asked a few more questions of Gigi before taking their leave. "If you think of anything else," Marcus said finally, "please don't hesitate to give us a call."

"I won't, Detective," Gigi promised as she shut her door behind them.

As the news sank in, she fed Max and peeled off her sweats. After a shower, she prepared coffee and sat down at the kitchen table, gazing out the window into her small garden. Sunlight streamed onto her rose bushes. Her neighbor, already busy in her backyard with her dachshund, waved enthusiastically. Gigi raised a hand in return and retreated from her window, suddenly grouchy.

That woman notices everything, she thought. *And that scrawny dog of hers belongs on a hot dog bun.*

She glanced appreciatively at Max and simultaneously regretted the fact that she was not a morning person. Unpleasant things usually happened in the morning, she reflected, as she reached for the telephone.

Cleo Cooper's voice sounded sleepy. "Hello?"

Gigi tried to smile. "Cleo? It's Gigi Ross. I'm sorry to bother you so early in the morning. I wanted to let you know that it won't be necessary to come into work today. The offices will be closed all week in light of recent events."

"I heard about Mr. Caxton," Cleo acknowledged. "Do you have any idea what happened?"

Gigi took a deep breath and told her about Brian's murder. It sounded as if Cleo, with a small yelp, had sat straight up in bed. "Mr. Chivas is dead, too? Omigod, I didn't see the news last night! I can't believe it! Why would someone want to kill them both?"

Gigi tried to stem the flow of words. "Cleo, I don't know. The police don't know. Mark told Brian everything; it's possible that they knew something that was too important to come out. I've scoured my brain to think of anything that's recently occurred at the office that might be relevant. I think you should do the same."

Cleo was already thinking. "Do you think we're in danger, too, working in the same office?" She said finally. "I've been thinking about a couple of things that the police might want to know about Mr. Caxton, but maybe we should put our heads together and see if we can come up with anything? You should be careful, Ms. Ross, maybe you're next."

After Gigi hung up the phone, she carefully got ready for the office, applying discreet make-up to her already flawless face and donning a slim dark suit. She picked sheer black stockings and sling-back heels. She had a few things to attend to at the Broad Street office and knew the media would be there waiting.

Despite her fondness for being the center of attention, Gigi was shocked by the media circus that awaited her in front of the offices of Caxton, Chivas & Ross. Reporters from as far away as Miami and Philadelphia were there; Gigi thought she glimpsed someone from CNN. She had no choice but to say a few words into the microphones thrust at her, acutely aware of the sticky patina of sensationalism that was settling on the event.

"Ladies and gentlemen," she began, trying to remember the salient facts, "I joined this architectural firm two years ago with high hopes for a fruitful partnership with two of the most promising architects the East Coast has recently produced. This weekend has changed my life immeasurably. With the untimely loss of both my partners, my future with this firm and in Charleston is uncertain. The office will be closed for the week, while we attempt to bring justice to bear in this tragic situation. I am hopeful that the person or persons responsible for this unprecedented circumstance will be brought swiftly to justice. On behalf of my partners' families and myself, I would ask for you to respect our privacy and help us through this difficult time. Thank you in advance."

Gigi escaped through the heavy double doors into the office building, leaving the inevitable barrage of questions hanging in the early morning air.

"Ms. Ross, do you know who murdered your partners?"
"Ms. Ross, do you stand to inherit the firm or the property owned by Caxton, Chivas & Ross?"
"Gigi, do you think you're next?"

* * * * *

Kate Caxton saw the throng of reporters and television cameras on Broad Street as she drove up East Bay toward the hospital. Her stomach was upset. Her chest hurt with every breath, as it always did when she was anxious. She had braved a few reporters herself as she left for work that morning, head bent and sunglasses on.

Safely inside her Mercedes, she had breathed a sigh of relief. Seeing patients in the clinic today would be hard enough, but at least her staff would be supportive, and the sympathy of her patients unlikely to reduce her to tears. She had thought about not going to work, about taking the week off, and, after the funeral tomorrow, leaving town for a few days. *Maybe a trip to Hilton Head with Laura to get my mind off of things would be a good idea,* Kate thought as she reached the hospital parking garage. *Maybe Melanie should come along, too*, she decided sadly, and felt tears forming.

Holding her head up high, she parked the car and let the morning breeze dry her eyes as she headed toward the hospital entrance. She knew herself well enough to know that the key, for her, was to stay busy. She did not believe in wallowing in the sympathy of others.

Her choice was a fortunate one, as the day was hectic. She saw an emergency patient with a retinal detachment and, using a model of an eyeball to explain the diagnosis, mechanically discussed the risks, benefits, and alternatives to surgery. The patient was visiting Charleston on vacation and made no mention of her husband's death. She signed him up for surgery on her operating room day, Wednesday. She saw several post-operative patients, as well as the usual quota of diabetics and older people with varying degrees of age-related macular degeneration. An explanation of the newest, non-thermal laser treatment for this condition was also a rote answer for her. Photodynamic therapy, she explained, was probably not yet the definitive answer to AMD, but it was successful in stabilizing disease in many patients and certainly the best option to date.

Kate worked through lunch and finished her clinic early, at four o'clock. She had been waiting for this moment.

Sitting in a quiet corner of the clinic, she picked up a frequently-used telephone and dialed. The low-level murmur of the techs in the distance, talking about everything from the newest diet fad to the latest in body glitter, faded as the receiver was picked up.

"Hello?" The voice was young and deep, distinctly male.

Kate's voice was as soft as the look in her eyes. "Hi, it's me."

* * * * *

Earlier that afternoon, Gigi had had enough. She was sick of the office, sick of reporters, sick of Charleston. Slipping into jeans, she loaded an excited Max into the Range Rover and left for Hilton Head. She would try some retail therapy, she told herself.

Stopping by her bank, First Federal of Charleston, almost directly opposite the architectural firm, Gigi withdrew five thousand dollars. She had long ago learned to counteract her expensive tastes by paying for everything in cash. She owned just one credit card and that was for emergencies. Tucking the money away, and not even certain she would need it, she took Broad Street west to Lockwood Drive and got onto the old bridge leading into West Ashley.

Following Savannah Highway west, Gigi passed the motels and car dealerships that populate that last stretch of Highway 17 before it begins to melt into countryside dotted with marshland and old plantation homes. Ancient oak trees hung with Spanish moss led the way to Walterboro and then Beaufort. Fiddling with the radio, Gigi began to sing along as an old Neil Diamond tune began. *September morn, we danced until the night became a brand new day, two lovers playing scenes from some romantic play, September morning still can make me feel that way...*

After a brief stint on I-95, Gigi took the first exit for Hilton Head and found herself on a picturesque road with woods on either side, an occasional white-pillared home peeking through the trees. She stopped at a vegetable stand and bought fresh tomatoes and boiled peanuts, a delicacy peculiar to the South, to which she and Max had both become addicted.

With her dog munching happily in the back seat, Gigi began to improvise to Roy Orbison. *Pretty woman, driving down the street, pretty woman, the kind you'd like to meet...*

Suddenly, a sleek Porsche Carrera tried to pass her on the narrow road. Instinctively, Gigi took her foot off the accelerator until she noticed the large truck bearing down in the opposite lane. She braked; the Porsche squeezed past her in a flourish of silver and a loud honk. It disappeared in a cloud of dust.

Some miles later, Gigi turned onto Hilton Head Highway, soon crossing the majestic bridge onto the island and keeping an eye out for the low-slung, red-roofed outlet stores on her right. She found them soon enough, parked the car and, attaching Max to a leash, began to walk in the bright sunshine past Nine West, Maidenform, and Eddie Bauer. It felt good to be away from the city. The air was briny; she imagined that she could already hear the sound of the sea. Perhaps after finishing her shopping, she would have a facial at one of the island spas before returning to Charleston. Gigi took a deep breath and felt some of the tension of the last days leave her body.

Outside the Clinique store, she caught sight of the Porsche from the road pulling into a parking lot. Gigi watched as a tall, dark-haired man emerged from the car and began walking toward the store. He saw her standing there watching him and bent to pat Max, who, settled on his haunches with his tongue hanging out in a doggy smile, was on his best behavior.

"Hey, buddy," the man crooned. "I recognize this furry face from the road." He smiled as he rubbed Max's neck and looked up at Gigi.

"Thanks for saving me out there a while back. I would've been road kill if you hadn't slowed down."

Gigi found herself smiling back. "I thought the car was familiar. I used to have one of those myself, and I certainly remember my days of needing to go too fast in that thing."

The man straightened up. Max whined. "What happened to yours? Were you in a wreck?"

"No," Gigi sighed. "I got my dog. His name is Max. And he seems to have fallen in love with you."

Twenty minutes later, the two were browsing through the Calvin Klein store with Max lying in the shade of a palmetto tree outside. Jack Citron was a lawyer from Atlanta on his way to golf with friends at Sea Pines. Gigi found him to be interesting, funny, considerate, and very sexy. She thought she saw interest reflected in his eyes as she tried on a few evening gowns and modeled for him in front of the three-way mirror. She was not surprised when he suggested dinner at one of the Sea Pines restaurants.

Since Max would not fit into the sports car, they took two cars and soon were seated outside at Anthony's, chardonnay in hand and Max sleeping at their feet. A view of the sunset was imminent, and the gleam in Jack's eye was unmistakable. They talked through spinach salad appetizers —garnished with fresh tomato, red onion, and feta cheese— and the seafood that followed. Jack, apparently an aficionado of heart-healthy dishes, had grilled mahi-mahi, while Gigi tried the sweet potato-encrusted tuna.

"Wow, this is really excellent," she exclaimed. "I'm from New York, where we don't really consider tuna to have that much potential."

Jack grinned. "This is my favorite restaurant on the island. No matter what you order, you can't go wrong." He refilled her wine glass.

"So, when are you meeting your friends?" Gigi changed the subject after they ordered coffee, pulling their chairs together so they could both view the sunset. The espresso was warm in her hand. She was keenly aware of Jack's linen sleeve brushing her arm and the things he could give her.

"Not until tomorrow morning," he acknowledged. "Hank owns the condo, he's arriving tomorrow afternoon, and the other two are getting in sometime after breakfast. We've all been buddies since law school and take a week every quarter for some R & R."

Gigi wondered how often women were included on the schedule. She had no illusions that she was the first or that she would be the last. She let Jack pay the bill and left the restaurant with him.

Outside, Jack tucked her arm through his and took Max's leash. "We're close to the condo already. Want to walk over and enjoy the sunset?"

"Sure," Gigi said. "You're a pretty romantic guy."

* * * * *

By the time Kate finished her dictations—in these days of managed care, it was not only a nicety but a necessity to send letters back to the referring docs—it was almost dark outside. Her thoughts veered to Melanie who, she knew, was suffering much more than she was herself. She decided to check in on her friend. *I'll wear my white coat, act like I know what I'm doing, and no one will tell me I can't see her,* she thought. *Maybe they'll discharge her, and I can take her home with me, poor thing.*

She checked her e-mail and sent a reply to one of Mark's sisters, who was finalizing the details of Mark's funeral tomorrow morning at St. Philip's.

I agree, white roses will be beautiful.

Swallowing the lump in her throat, Kate grabbed her briefcase and passed through her secretary's office. This was an antechamber to her own, and she saw that another flower arrangement had been left on Tricia's desk. She checked the card—with deepest sympathy from the Gallaghers—and left them on the desk. *Maybe I don't deserve all this sympathy,* she thought.

Kate had no difficulty finding Melanie, who was tucked away on the parquet-covered ninth floor amongst the cardiac patients. A quick call to Bed Control had settled that question. Two police officers were seated outside her room, but they parted like the Red Sea at the sight of Kate's white coat. She signed her name in the police log, and one officer accompanied her in to see her friend.

"Kate!" Melanie was clearly happy to see her and did not appear sedated. She hugged her friend and wiped her eyes.

"Well, who would've thought we'd end up like this?" Melanie said, her eyes bright with tears. "We've got to figure out what's going on. And will you help me get out of here?" She grimaced. "There were no beds except up here, and the arrhythmia monitors go off all the time. I've never been in the hospital, and this isn't the time to start."

Kate turned to the cop keeping watch inside the room. "Could we have a few minutes alone?" she asked, hoping the authority of her white coat had some effect on the officer. "I promise I won't be long."

The officer reluctantly left the room, but not before warning the women that they only had five minutes. He had been left with strict instructions to watch over this patient; he wasn't about to get in trouble while they had a tea party, doctor or no doctor.

Melanie and Kate waited for the door to close behind the officer before continuing their conversation. Melanie was such a wild-eyed patient that Kate almost laughed. She made a quick telephone call to the admitting doctor, who remembered her from her internship days, and Melanie was released to her care. As she got dressed, the friends speculated on the recent events.

"I have no idea what's going on," Melanie admitted as she pulled on a powder blue sweater and black pants, along with her favorite boots, dropped off earlier by Amanda. "There's got to be a connection from the office, don't you think?"

Kate was thoughtful. "Well, if I didn't do it, and you didn't do it, who does that leave?" She counted on her fingers. "Their partner, Gigi, or their business rival, Grimke."

"Hey, you could help Laura with her next novel," Melanie smiled. "How about other people at the office? Maybe we should investigate their new secretary, or maybe it's connected with the Palmetto Pointe contract." She sighed, trying to comb her unruly mop of dark hair with her fingers. "Gosh, I wish I'd listened more when Brian discussed the office. I was always so wrapped up in the gallery, I never really paid attention."

Kate said, "I hadn't really thought about it, but it seems like Mark used to talk about work a lot more. It seems like over the last few months he didn't want to bother me with it." She paused. "Mellie, what about Amanda? I think she's sweet, but maybe still a little bit in love with Mark? What was she doing last night?"

Melanie suddenly became intent on rooting through her capacious purse. She found a creamy foundation stick and powdered her nose and face in ivory, then applied a swipe of lipstick before glancing around the room one last time. "I think I have everything," she said.

As if on cue, the nurse came in to discuss discharge orders. Kate only half-listened as she watched her friend accept a prescription for a sedative and sign her name on the bottom of the release form.

Is Melanie hiding something about Amanda?

11

Cleo Cooper squeezed into a sequined tank top and surveyed herself critically in the full-length mirror.

It was eight o'clock. She was going to take advantage of her unexpected week of vacation by going out with a girlfriend. Too pumped to care that at the end of her vacation she might not have a job, she added black velvet pants and strappy platform heels to complete the outfit. She turned attention to her face. Cleo carefully blended a layer of foundation, then added mascara and bright lipstick, which emphasized her already generous mouth. After applying a glittery lotion that sparkled on her shoulders and cleavage, she was fiddling with her hair when the telephone rang.

She hoped it wasn't Joey. They had had a fight and she didn't want to cancel her girls' night out, not even for the great make-up sex they usually had. "Hello?"

"Hey, it's me." Her friend Tracy sounded as though she had already had a drink or two. "Should I come over there, or do you wanna meet me at Wet Willie's?" They often met at their favorite bar on East Bay Street, near the Market.

"What're you wearing?" Cleo listened as Tracy described boot-cut black jeans, a metallic lime-green bustier, and her favorite leather jacket, then nodded. "I'll meet you at Willie's, I'm leaving now." She slipped her cell phone and cigarettes into her purse and headed to the door.

An hour later, they had long since abandoned the bar for the livelier dance scene at Level 2, a funky club on the north side of Market Street. Cleo, clearly enjoying herself, was dancing with a stranger. Through the smoky haze, he introduced himself.

"I'm Kyle," he started. "My uncle lives here in Charleston; I'm staying out at his beach house on Folly for a couple of months. I hope to intern with him early in the new year."

"What does your uncle do?" She thought about some of the nicer homes on Folly Beach, just southwest of the Charleston peninsula. This guy had potential.

"He's an architect," Kyle said. He casually raised his beer to his lips and took a long swallow.

For some reason, Cleo felt a tiny frisson of fear. She wished she weren't quite so drunk and stared back at the man in front of her. "Really. Which one?"

"I think he's pretty well known," Kyle said, leading her off the dance floor and over to a dark corner table. "His name's Grimke, Luke Grimke. He's my mom's brother, originally from—"

"San Francisco," Cleo finished the sentence.

"Yeah," Kyle glanced at her appreciatively. "You know him?"

She nodded. "Yeah, I work for the other big architectural firm in town, Caxton, Chivas & Ross," she admitted. "Actually, they're not so big anymore. Two of 'em just died this weekend." The words sounded odd as Cleo said them, but Kyle just nodded.

"Yeah, I saw that on TV," he said soberly. "Uncle Luke feels terrible because they were both friends of his, he says. Hey, I guess you knew them pretty well, too. I'm sorry."

Cleo shrugged, not wanting the moment to turn gloomy. "Yeah, well, I only worked there for two months. The big question now is who did it, and what'll happen to the remaining partner. She's from New York City; I don't really think she likes the South very much."

"Wow, what's not to like?" Perhaps sensing her discomfort, Kyle deftly changed the subject. "Gorgeous weather, palm trees on every corner, the beach, the sunshine, beautiful women..." His eyes lingered on Cleo's face.

"Maybe she doesn't like the competition." Cleo laughed; Kyle seemed to appreciate her sense of humor. A few minutes later, she waved to Tracy through the throng of people as they left the club.

The night air was moist. Kyle's hand was steady on the wheel of the Mustang convertible he drove. His other hand was warm on Cleo's thigh. They drove down Calhoun street and took the new bridge, familiarly known as the Connector, to James Island. Taking a left turn onto Folly Road, Kyle drove a bit too fast down the strip, passing Wal-Mart and Mariner's Cay. When he reached the end of the road, with the Holiday Inn in front of them, he turned right and soon pulled into the oyster shell driveway of a beachfront house balanced on stilts. They parked under the house, in an open-air garage, and he helped her up the stairs, which took them into the kitchen.

"Gosh, this is gorgeous!" Cleo exclaimed as she walked into the living room, which was all windows and polished parquet, set off to maximum advantage by soft furniture and throw rugs.

She sank onto a linen-covered sofa and giggled as Kyle came to join her, carrying another beer. He put his arm around her; she turned her face toward his for a kiss.

* * * * *

Kate and Melanie, in sunglasses, sat in a booth at Pusser's Landing, a restaurant near the hospital that was located next to the marina. They had come not so much to eat as to talk, aware that the media, not to mention the police, beset their homes. Melanie picked at her salad, while

Kate tried to finish the she-crab soup she had ordered. Today she thought the dark sherry lacing the traditional Charleston dish looked like blood.

Kate spoke first. "I just got an e-mail from Mark's sister. The funeral is all set for tomorrow, eleven o'clock at St. Philip's." The Church Street structure, for which the street is named, is a Charleston landmark, recently renovated after sustaining significant damage during Hurricane Hugo in 1989.

"She's sweet to realize you couldn't handle that all alone," Melanie commented. "Do all of his sisters still live in Charleston?"

"Actually, two are in Atlanta, and Candace is in Beaufort. I don't really know that much about them. His parents died in the mid-eighties, I think, shortly after he and Brian moved back to Charleston." She looked sympathetically at her friend. "Honey, what are you going to do about Brian's funeral?"

Melanie started to weep. "Oh, God, I don't know, he doesn't have much family left. His parents were only children; they're dead now. Brian has just one brother." She blew her nose and looked at her friend. "I guess I'll arrange something at St. Philip's, too, maybe for Friday."

Kate reached over for Melanie's hand. "Don't worry, we'll get it done. Maybe after it's all over, we can go down to the islands, or something, just to get away. Laura was already suggesting a spa somewhere. I think she has the right idea. We could all go together, maybe even Amanda could come." She watched Melanie's face, hidden behind her sunglasses.

Melanie was quiet for a moment, then spoke in a rush. "Oh, Kate, I don't know if it means anything, but Amanda was at the Harris Teeter last night; we ran into her. Then I think I remember her face outside in the rain after I found Brian. She never came over to me, never said a word, just stood there, watching."

Kate tried not to show her surprise. Amanda, on the scene of the crime? Where had she been at the time of Mark's death? "Honey, I think you're overreacting. It's the shock. She probably heard you saying you needed to pick up some stuff; it put the idea into her head. Doesn't the gallery close at nine o'clock on Sundays through September? She probably decided to go get a few things after she locked up there."

"Yes, that's true," but Melanie did not seem comforted. She seemed about to say something, apparently thought better of it, and spoke next about the gallery. "We're closing the gallery for the rest of the week. It's just not fair to have Amanda do so much by herself; I've been so unreliable lately." She sniffled.

"We could all use a break," Kate agreed, as their waitress brought coffee. "I know it's a lot to think about right now, but we need to realize that it's unlikely that all this was done randomly. Melanie, do you realize someone we know probably killed our husbands?"

* * * * *

Over Kate's objections, Melanie insisted on being dropped off at her own home and spending the night alone. Kate was frank about her disapproval.

"Brian was still with us less than twenty-four hours ago! You can't possibly be ready to be left alone so soon. Even if you feel like you can handle it now, remember how different it's going to be when you walk into that home you two shared. Why don't you stay with me tonight?"

But Melanie was shaking her head. "I need to be alone, Kate," she replied. "I'm fine. The house was mine, mine and Domino's long before Brian joined us. I need to get back in touch with me, and I have to do it by myself." She shook her head. "I'm sorry, because I know you could use the company, too, but solitude is everything to me at a time like this."

"But you're the most people-loving person I know!" Kate was at a loss. "Anyway, your doctor discharged you to my care." She was only half-joking. "How can I just leave you alone when you're going through a nightmare?"

Melanie gave her a watery smile. "I'm going to be fine. I'll be fine. I appreciated Brian every day he was mine. Perfect things never last forever. I think, deep down, we both knew that. He wouldn't want me to be sad." She hugged her friend. "Look, I'll call you first thing in the morning, okay? We'll go to the church together."

Reluctantly, Kate agreed. She had no choice. "Well, okay, but call me if you need anything. Try the cell phone if I'm not home. I can be here in two minutes." She gave Melanie another hug, eyeing her friend with concern, then watched as Melanie unlocked the white door of her Tradd Street home, its pale blue exterior looking gray in the darkness.

The house had been meticulously restored to include flowers in the original holders beneath the two first floor windows and a semicircular, wrought iron balcony on the second floor outside the master bedroom. The lot on the eastern side of the house was empty, its historic home having been lost in a fire a long time ago. In the morning, Melanie's rooms were filled with sun. But now, late at night, the drawing room and living room with its grand staircase, as well as the big bedrooms upstairs, were all dark. Kate pictured her friend stepping into the small marbled entryway and climbing the two steps into the drawing room. Her Charleston single home, so called because it was just one room wide, was large enough to hold many memories.

I hope she knows what she's doing, Kate thought as she pulled away and took a right onto East Bay Street. *She's all alone now.* She sighed and drove slowly home. It was just a few short blocks to Lamont Street, and she was pleased to see neither reporters nor police lying in wait. She parked on the street and went inside her own empty house.

Her home, a bungalow, was not a traditional Charleston house. It was not a single and did not have the west- or south-facing balcony that early Charlestonians had constructed to bring in breezes from the ocean and ward off malaria-laden mosquitoes. Sometimes Kate wished for such an outside refuge. Its traditionally light-blue painted ceiling supposedly kept ghosts and other spirits at bay. Charleston residents, not immune to the mysteries of their historic city, still placated the spirits in such a fashion.

Or maybe it's just tradition, like Charleston Red in the drawing rooms. Whatever, ghost tours sure are a popular tourist attraction, Kate reflected as she entered her living room and immediately switched on a sofa-side lamp. A warm glow suffused the room, but the golden light did not extend to the glass-roofed sun room that lined the west side of the house, connected to both living room and kitchen by arched doorways, nor did it extend to the staircase or the east hallway leading to the study beyond.

Kate shivered with a sudden chill. *We loved each other so much at one time, Mark*, she thought. *What happened?*

She tossed her jacket onto the overstuffed sofa and walked across the honey-hued wooden floor to the kitchen. While she waited for water to boil, she sat at the kitchen table, a massive affair custom-made to fit the northern side of the house and curve around toward the sun room. The small garden and patio that their landscaper had put in the first year they moved into the house was swathed in shadow.

Again, Kate was pricked by uneasiness, as if a set of eyes were secretly following her face in the darkness. Abruptly, she got up to lower the blinds and felt better after a warm mug of tea was in her hands.

Kicking off her shoes and peeling off the stockings and skirt in which she had gone through her day, Kate stood in her underwear in the middle of the kitchen, contemplating her next move. She considered a bubble bath with the newest issue of *Archives of Ophthalmology* for company, but after a moment moved instead into the little laundry room with its adjacent bath, which was neatly built under the staircase. Finding her favorite jeans, she slipped them on and took her tea out into the living room.

Darkness stared in from the windows here as well. After pulling all the shades closed, Kate settled into Mark's favorite armchair, strategically placed to afford an optimal view of the television, his one concession to his former life as a sports-obsessed bachelor. Kate settled into the depths of the chair, pulling an old velvet throw around her shoulders and tucking her feet under her instead of using the footstool that Mark, with his long legs, had always favored. The chair was big enough for two; she remembered many nights squeezing into it with him, warm and safe and happy.

We really went our separate ways a while ago, she thought. *If I had thought he still loved me, I would never have...* Her thoughts stopped short as the telephone rang. She let the answering machine pick it up and was shocked to hear Mark's voice reverberate through the house.

"Hello, you've reached Mark and Katharine Caxton.

We're off somewhere having fun, so leave a message, we'll call you back." *He sounds like he's smiling,* Kate thought as she remembered the rainy afternoon more than two years ago when they had finally moved in and were feeling as if it was their house. She remembered the look in his eyes as he finished recording that message and put his arms around her. *Welcome home, honey,* he had said, and they had been so proud of themselves, with their new home and their new life together. They had made love right there on the living room floor.

Kate sighed as no one left a message. A soft click was the only sound she heard. *Oh Mark,* she thought. *I'm sorry, I'm sorry, I'm sorry, it didn't turn out the way we thought...*

* * * * *

Cleo untangled her legs from the sheet and quietly got out of the bed. Kyle, naked and snoring, lay on his stomach, his hair spiky against the edge of the pillow. The green glow of a night light plugged in next to the louvered doors leading to the bath illuminated his well-muscled body. Through an alcohol-induced haze, Cleo vaguely remembered the events of the evening.

In the darkened room, she looked around for a clock, but could not find one. Her contact lenses were sticky under her eyelids, and she had to pee. Deciding that she was in no hurry to get home, since she had the week off, Cleo made her way into the tiled bath. The lines of the modern house were sleek and expensive. Cleo noticed that the bathroom was tiled in a deep bottle green, and the towels were pure white. She flushed the toilet; it hardly made a sound. She peered into a grotto-like shower, also tiled in the color of the ocean depths. Washing her hands in the marble sink, she leaned forward to inspect her pallid face. Her eyes were red, and she saw black smudges from her mascara. It wasn't supposed to smudge, but of course it always did. She tried to remember what cosmetics she had put into her evening case. If Kyle woke up, she would have to repair her face.

Drying her hands on a perfect white towel, she ventured into the bedroom again. Kyle lay as before. Cleo picked up his denim shirt and slipped it on, preparing to find the living room and her evening bag. She hoped she had remembered concealer.

She stepped carefully into the sunken living room, suddenly grateful for her scant clothing, as the floor-to-ceiling windows were uncovered. Outside she could see the dark silhouette of palmetto trees leading to the beach. A golden glow from a subterranean floodlight illuminated the sunken pool; she suddenly remembered Kyle making love to her in the warm water before taking her into the bedroom.

Just as she was reaching for her purse, a sudden movement caught Cleo's eye. Was that a person edging carefully through the garden, or was it just her imagination? Cleo's heart was pounding, and her eyes felt gritty. She blinked rapidly, trying to restore the tear film on her contact lenses. She really should stop sleeping with her lenses in. Maybe she should get that new laser surgery for nearsightedness, what was it called? *Oh yeah, LASIK,* Cleo thought as she squinted outside, her gaze pinned on the palmetto tree nearest the pool. She couldn't see anything anymore. Maybe it had been one of the neighborhood cats on the prowl.

Heart still thudding, Cleo grabbed her bag and was just taking out her makeup remover when a small sound caught her attention. *What is that?* It sounded like a finger tapping gently on the glass window. She looked up and felt a ripple of fear go down her spine as she saw a figure standing just outside the French windows. Then she recognized the face looking at her.

Relief washed over her as she hurried to the front door. It was a large double-wide oak door that she unlocked with trembling hands. Her visitor was inside the entryway in a moment.

"What are you doing here?" Cleo was curious, but not suspicious. She noticed that her visitor was wearing dark gloves on this warm summer night, but was too surprised to make a sound when, suddenly, the hands were wrapped around her throat, squeezing, tighter and tighter. She tried to struggle, to scream, but had to concentrate instead on drawing her last breath.

Gray shapes circled in front of her eyes, and then an explosion of bright light was followed by unrelenting blackness.

12

Gigi awoke on Tuesday morning feeling exhausted, physically and emotionally. She had driven back from Hilton Head in the middle of the night, Max next to her, suddenly unable to stay with Jack for a moment longer.

Their lovemaking had been routine. He had let her into the condo and offered her another drink first taking her coat and settling her on the sofa. Max remained outside.

She had turned down the drink, and his bourbon had remained untasted on the counter because she had come over to him and started unbuttoning her blouse. His eyes on her breasts, he unzipped his pants; they did it standing up, right there in the living room, with him entering her from behind. Then they went into the bedroom, where he watched television, and she watched him, until he wanted to do it again. He came inside her twice more before falling asleep, one leg pinning her to the bed. She was sticky and uncomfortable; and the room was too cold.

Unable to fall asleep, she finally got out from under him and dressed in the living room where all her clothes were. He did not awaken. She left without saying goodbye.

Max seemed relieved to see her.

Now, in the early dawn, she was unsure of the void she was trying to fill. She only knew she had been unsuccessful.

* * * * *

There is a little westward curve in Church Street, right

where St. Philip's Church is. Otherwise, the street, one of the most picturesque in Charleston, runs in straight segments from Pinckney Street, north of the Market, down to South Battery where it ends at White Point Gardens.

Laura knew this because she walked from Fort Sumter House through the Gardens and up Church Street for Mark's funeral. It was a perfect day, cool and sunny, without the humidity or the threat of rain that had plagued the coastal city until several days ago.

She was not the first to arrive for the funeral. Kate was already there, with Mark's three sisters at her side. Candace, Claire, and Camille, nee Caxton, all resembled their younger brother. They were tall, dark, lean, and in control. Kate gave Laura a tearful hug, but there appeared to be some color in her cheeks. Laura thought she looked remarkably calm for a woman unexpectedly having to bury her husband. She offered her condolences and sat down next to Melanie, who looked as awful as would have been expected. Her dark hair had lost its curl. Her face was so pale it appeared translucent in the sun-filled chapel. Laura slipped an arm around her frail shoulders. She did not know Melanie very well, but that suddenly seemed irrelevant. *We are all allies in the face of death, the great equalizer*, she thought.

"How are you doing?" The question seemed silly in its obviousness, but Melanie looked relieved at the diversion.

"I'm better, thanks," she actually sounded as though she meant it. "I had some time last night to sort through things and get everything straight in my head." She half-turned and spoke very softly in Laura's ear, gripping her hand so tightly the circulation almost stopped. "It's simple. If I find the son of a bitch who killed my husband, I'll destroy him."

Or her, Laura added mentally but left the thought unspoken.

She glanced around at the other people who had come to pay their respects. She saw a distinguished-looking older man with gray hair and strikingly blue eyes and recognized Luke Grimke from his recent photograph in the newspaper. His face was unsmiling as he bent his head to listen to the words of the elegant, silver-haired woman next to him. Laura wondered if she was his wife. They sat down in the pew behind her, his hand in hers. Just as Laura noticed a wraith-like Amanda entering the church, a voice spoke next to her.

"Melanie, honey, how are you doing?" Melanie's reply was muffled as she stood up and hugged the newcomer, a tall woman whose auburn hair was set off to maximum advantage by the dove gray suit she wore. She also sported demure little diamond stud earrings, but no other jewelry, and her eyes were rimmed in red. "I'm so sorry about Brian, if there's anything I can do, anything, I hope you'll let me know."

"Thank you so much," Melanie seemed grateful for the support and made introductions. "Laura, this is Gigi Ross, Brian and Mark's business partner. Gigi, Laura Lindross, a friend of Kate's who's recently moved to Charleston."

Laura surveyed Gigi with interest and was impressed by her warm, firm handshake. She thought she heard a hint of a southern drawl. "Nice to meet you, Laura, I'm just sorry it had to be under these circumstances. How recently have you moved to Charleston?"

"I got here last month," Laura acknowledged and found herself smiling in response to Gigi's wry expression.

"Well, I hope you're not too put off by the events of the week," Gigi said. "I can assure you, the city is usually much more civilized!"

As the organ music became louder, the three women

resumed their seats. Kate sat down in the front row, Mark's sisters next to her. The low murmur of voices continued for a few minutes, and then Chopin's austere and beautiful funeral march began. Everyone stood as the minister came to the pulpit. Mark's polished mahogany coffin was covered with white roses that matched those arranged throughout the chapel. The music stopped; as the last chords died away, the silence became complete.

"Beloved," the minister began. "We are gathered here today in the sight of God to celebrate the life of Marcus Michael Caxton, our husband, brother, uncle, and friend who was taken from this world too soon."

Okay, so this is pretty grim, Laura thought, grateful for the good health of her family and friends and her relative immunity to the grief that pervaded the room. She simply had not known the man very well. She became aware of sobbing nearby and saw shaking shoulders in front of her. Long champagne-colored hair spilled over a black cashmere sweater. As the woman turned to accept a tissue from the person next to her, Laura recognized Amanda Michaels. *She should have come to sit with us,* Laura thought. *I wonder why she sat alone?*

"While we do not question your wisdom, O Lord, nor your beneficent spirit, we do ask the opportunity to reflect on the gifts that Mark gave to this world and the beauty that he left behind."

Next to Laura, Melanie was overtaken with emotion. Finally, she got the words out. "This should have been Brian, giving eulogy for his best friend," she sobbed. "I can't believe they're both gone."

Gently rocking the woman back and forth, Laura listened to the several eulogies, made by a sister, college friends, and business associates. She was impressed when

Luke rose and spoke. Gigi also contained her grief and got out a few words before tears threatened to overtake her. Laura could not help but wonder whether either of them had killed Mark and Brian. It seemed ludicrous, but how could a double murder like this be random?

"Dear Lord, we ask that you take your child, Mark, into your Kingdom, where all pain is assuaged, all grief is vanquished, all wrong is made right, and hope is everlasting."

Silence fell in the church. Dust motes, illuminated by a shaft of summer light, danced above Mark's coffin. The congregation sat with bowed heads.

Just before the organ music began again, a cell phone rang. Disapproving eyes fastened on Luke Grimke as he hastily extracted his cellular phone and hunched forward in his seat.

"Hello?" He tried to speak softly, his embarrassment evident, but Laura could not help but catch the trail of words directly behind her.

"Kyle? Kyle, get a grip on yourself, get a grip. I can't understand a word you're saying! What's happened? What? Dead? Someone's dead? Unbelievable, I can't be hearing you right. Are you sure she's dead? Yes, absolutely, I'm on my way."

* * * * *

Luke grimly hung on to the steering wheel as he screeched around a corner.

His thoughts were a mass of confused impressions and nightmarish anticipation. Kyle was a good kid, the best, he reflected. Like a son to him. Perhaps he just thought the girl was dead, she might be drunk or sulking, trying to scare him. What the hell was she doing there anyway? Kyle hadn't been in town long enough to be dating anyone seriously. *Goddamn kid, can't even keep his pants zipped for ten minutes. I'm gonna crucify that son of a bitch for calling me in the middle of that funeral, as if I don't have enough things to worry about already.* Luke's thoughts careened around like his car as he swerved onto the beach house driveway and skidded to a stop.

He hurried up the walk, then came to a stop as he saw Kyle standing on the weathered steps. The two men looked at each other. Kyle spoke first.

"It looks as if whoever...did this to her came in the front door," he spoke matter-of-factly. "Maybe we'd better go in the pool entrance, that's how I got out."

Luke allowed himself to be led around the side of the building, up a sandy slope and through the wooden, planked door to the enclosed pool. Everything looked normal to him. The bungalow's French windows, just beyond the pool, were open. Kyle hung back. Luke advanced slowly. As he stepped over the threshold into the living room, it took his eyes a moment to adjust to the darkness. Then he made out a shapeless form lying just inside the entryway of the living room. Naked, rather chubby legs were sprawled over the parquet floor and a denim shirt covered the girl's backside. Hair that was obviously bleached was spread like a halo around a face that looked away from him. One plump hand, its nails polished a metallic shade, was flung out from her side as if she had just delivered the punch line to a well-received joke. The other arm appeared to be tucked underneath her.

Luke was across the room in two quick strides. He reached over the body and felt for a pulse on her neck. He could not find one, but did notice something else.

"My God," he stared at the splotchy discoloration on

her neck that was visible in the gloom. "She's been strangled."

The police came in droves, or so it seemed to Luke. Kyle was polite, calmly shaking hands and giving coherent explanations to the many questions that were asked. Luke felt as if everything were moving in slow motion. He listened as his nephew related his side of the story.

"She seemed like a nice girl. We met downtown at Level 2 and danced together. I think she was with a friend; once or twice she got a call on her cell phone and had to go outside the bar to answer it. She seemed happy and excited; that's what made me notice her. I like light-hearted people; life's too short to be depressed, you know?" The irony of his statement came to him too late. He looked down at his hands, silent for a moment. "So, anyway, I asked her if she wanted to see the beach house; she knows Uncle Luke and was excited to see a place he had designed himself."

"She knows me?" Luke's voice sounded unnaturally loud to him.

"Well, she knew you," Kyle corrected himself quietly. "She said she worked for that other architectural firm in town, you know, the one with the two guys who've been offed lately." Kyle's face was suddenly chalk-white under his tan. "Oh my God, they killed her too."

Some moments later, Kyle was able to continue his narrative. "We drove out in my car. I think she must have walked downtown, she didn't say anything about her car, and when we got here I gave her a little tour before we, uh, before we, uh, settled in for the night."

Detective Marcus, called in on his day off, was not feeling charitable. "And what exactly did that settling in involve?"

Kyle, with a trace of embarrassment, detailed their

lovemaking in the pool and bedroom. "We were probably asleep well before midnight. I'm a pretty sound sleeper and didn't wake up until about eleven this morning. She wasn't in bed anymore, and I didn't hear her in the bathroom. But I could see her clothes in the living room. I thought she'd gotten up to make coffee or something." He swallowed. "So I took a shower and wandered out there, you know, that's when I saw her lying up against the wall of the entry hall. I didn't touch her, except on her left wrist to feel for a pulse. She was cold, you know, real cold, and I knew I wouldn't find a heartbeat. I didn't move her, but I kinda freaked out and called my uncle who said not to do anything until he got here." Kyle looked questioningly at Luke, who nodded. "Then I went outside. I used the French doors on the side of the house, so I wouldn't have to step over her body and drop...fibers and things. And I waited for my uncle on the steps out front."

Kyle's statements were carefully written down; after the final question was answered, Marcus addressed Luke.

"Can you tell me where you were between nine and two last night?"

Luke responded quickly. "I spent the evening at the house of a lady friend, Veronica Parker. Then I drove home around midnight. I answered some e-mails and other correspondence, had a brandy, and went to bed at about one o'clock. Ms. Parker can verify my whereabouts if necessary, I'm sure." He nodded slightly, as if signaling an end to the conversation.

Marcus was not dissuaded that quickly. "Did you know the deceased at all, Mr. Grimke?"

Luke shook his head. "No, I never met her. I guess I must have spoken with her on the telephone a couple of times, when I called the Caxton, Chivas & Ross offices, but I didn't know her. I guess she'd been their secretary for just a short time." He remembered the somewhat nasal voice that had answered the telephone when he had called the office just last week. She had sounded so young.

When the police were done with them, uncle and nephew sat outside on the terrace overlooking the ocean while the crime scene was investigated further. It was late September, and, in the warm weather, more than a few bathers were out on the sand. The waters of the Atlantic sparkled in the sun.

There was nothing to say.

* * * * *

Kate had reserved the Barbados Room at the Mills House for a brunch following the funeral. The sunken dining room had a courtyard terrace, easily visible though open French windows, and its two carpeted rooms were partially separated by columns atop waist-high walls. The illusion of depth was augmented by the mirrored back wall that reflected the patrons, the tuxedoed piano player, and the potted ferns scattered here and there on the courtyard slate.

Today, as always, this most sumptuous buffet in Charleston boasted a chef to make omelets and another to carve the roast beef. Fresh fruit, including pineapple, melon, and strawberries, was laid out next to spinach salad and other mixed greens amidst an array of fresh garnishes such as peppers, tomatoes, cucumbers, onions, olives, mushrooms, bacon, as well as feta and cheddar cheese. A huge ice sculpture introduced fresh shrimp and the seafood bar, and a dozen silver-plated warmers held entrees ranging from poached salmon to pork medallions to jambalaya. The table nearest the door was weighed down with dessert tortes, including chocolate hazelnut cake and key lime pie. Vanilla ice cream waited in a silver tureen.

While others ate and commented on the food, Kate stood, her back to the sunlight, accepting murmurs of sympathy. Melanie stared sadly out the French windows. Amanda was nowhere to be seen.

Not far away, Laura watched them all. She couldn't help but think the killer had attended the funeral today. It couldn't be possible that these murders were random and committed by different people. But, who among them had the motive and the know-how? And what about this third death? Who was it? No one else seemed to have heard Luke's startled commentary. He had not reappeared. Laura noticed that the firm's secretary also remained a no-show. Well, maybe she hadn't been invited.

Laura was curious about the third victim because that death might be related to Mark and Brian's deaths. She decided to poke around the assembled grievers to see what she could find out.

Noticing Gigi leaving the seafood table, she sidled up alongside her. "I'm really sorry about everything you're going through, Gigi," Laura said.

"Oh, thanks," Gigi replied, somewhat absentmindedly, "but I think Kate and Melanie are the ones we need to worry about now."

"I agree," Laura replied, "but your life has changed a lot as well. You're the only partner left in the firm, right?"

"What are you insinuating?" Gigi arched a carefully groomed eyebrow.

Laura held her hands up in defense. "Nothing. I'm just thinking that you have a lot of decisions to make now that you are sole owner."

"I suppose I do have some things at the firm I need to

deal with directly," Gigi conceded thoughtfully, "and there are also issues to work out with Kate and Melanie. Fortunately, the buy-out procedures and company valuation are all spelled out in the partnership agreement. It's pretty cut and dried."

"What do you think you'll do?" Laura asked.

"I honestly don't know," Gigi sighed. "It just won't be the same working in Charleston without Mark and Brian. It will be so hard facing the office every day knowing they won't be there."

"At least you still have the secretary to keep track of the day-to-day affairs," Laura stated. Making an obvious visual sweep of the room, she added, "I would've thought she would have shown up to the funeral. Any idea where she could be?"

"Cleo? I have no idea. She's a sweet enough girl, but kind of spacy. I wouldn't be surprised if she forgot." Gigi shrugged and put down her plate. "I'm really sorry, Laura, but I must be going. I'd like to say good-bye to Kate before I leave."

Thoughtfully, Laura watched Gigi move away and then looked around, noticing the gathering was starting to break up. She decided it was a good time to take her leave as well. She didn't think she had learned much.

Gigi found Kate in the archway leading to the rest rooms. "Let me know what I can do to help you," she said, her green eyes sympathetic.

Kate clasped her hand. "Yes, of course, I will," she said, grateful for the older woman's warmth. "I appreciate your kind words at the service today. I think now we need to focus on Melanie. Her grief is much fresher than mine."

Gigi watched her through hooded eyes. "And it seems much deeper," she observed.

Kate felt a dull flush creep around her neck.

"You should watch yourself, honey, people might start wondering if you've been the best wife possible. I know I have."

Kate pulled herself together. "Don't you threaten me..."

The other woman smiled and moved in for a hug, her voice very soft in Kate's ear. "Oh, it's not a threat, honey, just think of it as a warning from a friend."

As Gigi moved into the rest room, Kate abruptly sat down on a yellow silk chaise upholstered in a fleur-de-lys pattern. Her chest felt as if there were a weight on it, and her breath came in uneven gasps. She knew that her face was pale, probably hard to miss against the contrast of her black dress.

Who else knows?

13

After leaving the Mills House, Laura went home, not sure of the proper etiquette. She caught sight of Gigi hugging Kate and figured if Kate needed her, she would call. Heading across Meeting Street, she enjoyed the picturesque cobblestones of Chalmers Street and turned down Church Street.

After greeting Henry at the desk in the lobby of Fort Sumter House, Laura took the elevator to her apartment without running into anyone else. This pleased her, and she inserted her key in the lock, looking forward to a quiet afternoon after the emotion of the morning.

She had just settled onto the sofa with a cup of coffee and yesterday's mail when the telephone rang. For a moment she was not sure who it was. Then she heard Kate's voice.

"Laura," Kate spoke so softly it was difficult to hear her. "I'm sorry to bother you, but I'm desperate and need to talk to someone. You're the only one I can trust. Would you mind terribly if I came over there? Please."

Laura could feel her anguish over the line. "Of course, you should come. I'll pick you up."

"No, thank you, I'll be over there in five minutes. Laura, thank you!" The line went dead.

Puzzled but intrigued, Laura replaced the receiver. *More grist for the mill*, she thought. Her next novel would be unbelievable.

Two hours later, she wished she had taken notes.

Kate wanted to discuss all the possible suspects in Mark's death. She suddenly seemed driven, as if there would be another death if they didn't solve the mystery that day.

Laura could not quite understand her frantic insistence, but was happy to keep the momentum going.

"Let's look at the list of suspects," Laura suggested and looked closely at her friend. "Although I think there's something you're not telling me, Kate, I don't think you did it, okay? Maybe someday you'll let me in on the secret, but right now let's leave it. What we discuss won't leave this room. Let's talk about motive and opportunity."

Their list included Melanie, Amanda, Gigi, Luke, and Cleo. Both women were unemotional and analytical as they discussed the options.

"Melanie Moore Chivas, thirty-eight, married to Brian Chivas. Recently widowed, had to be sedated in the hospital when she heard the news of his death. Marriage seemed very happy. Motive?" Kate shrugged. "I don't know, why would a woman kill her husband's business partner and then her husband? Somebody knew something, perhaps. Maybe she was having an affair, and Mark found out. She says she was in the gallery on Saturday morning, but can Amanda corroborate that? We'll have to find out. On Sunday night, she was certainly on the scene of the crime; Brian was very recently dead when the police showed up."

"But no murder weapon was found," Laura pointed out. "Unless she slipped it down a storm sewer or hid it in the car or the bushes. We'll have to check those things."

"What about other motives?" Kate wondered. "Was there any financial benefit to their deaths?" She paused. "I should know the answer to that."

"Who inherited Mark's part of the firm, you, his widow, or Brian, his partner?" Laura sucked in her breath. "Maybe that explains the order of the deaths. Melanie stood to inherit everything!"

But Kate was shaking her head. "If you go with that

reasoning, then Gigi should get it all as the surviving partner."

"No, maybe she wasn't full partner yet, was she?" Laura prodded. "They were partners for fifteen years, and she's a full partner after less than two years? I doubt it."

"I'll have to talk to our lawyer," Kate acknowledged. "Since we each made a substantial income, we kept our finances pretty separate. So, Melanie has opportunity, and she has motive. Who's next?"

"How about Amanda Michaels, thirty-four years old, never married, almost married Mark until you came on the scene, perfectly civil on every occasion, but somewhat aloof. Still waters run deep, I think." Laura waited.

"Motive?" Kate spoke matter-of-factly. "She was still in love with him and finally figured out he was never going to leave me. She killed him out of jealousy, figuring if she can't have him, no one can."

Kate's voice trailed off as she looked at Laura. Her eyes filled with tears. "Laura, you know what? I think Mark was having an affair. Whether it was Amanda or someone else, I don't know. We just stopped talking. It had been that way for almost a year." She seemed to be trying to remember. "He stopped talking about work, and we never really made plans anymore, just the two of us. It's like he was already gone before he was even dead."

Laura was surprised. "Are you sure? And do you have proof it was Amanda?"

Kate shook her head. "No, it was just a feeling I had."

The two women were silent for a few moments. Kate seemed disinclined to speculate further on her revelation.

"Well, what about other motives?" Laura thought Kate was thankful for the change in subject. "Maybe Amanda had to kill her business partner's husband for some obscure reason, again, financial gain perhaps? And Mark's death was not the beginning of everything, just first in the time line."

"What about opportunity?" Kate wondered. "Again, we'll have to verify she was at the gallery with Melanie on Saturday morning. But she definitely had opportunity Sunday night; she was right there at the Harris Teeter."

"But admits it," Laura pointed out. She thought for a moment, then shrugged. "I'm not sure what that means, but I definitely think it's odd. Coincidences like that don't really happen." She grinned, "except in my novels."

"So, motive and opportunity both for Amanda, pending further investigation." Kate held up two fingers. "What about Gigi? Georgiana Gisele Ross, age forty-one, wannabe Southerner, but now talking about moving back home to New York City after the double murder of her partners. Is she heartbroken, terrified, or getting out while she can?"

"Hmm, I don't know her well, it could be any of the above," Laura conceded. "She seems kind of bitchy, but I also think she's very bright, and her heart's probably in the right place. What about motive?"

Kate considered. "It could definitely be financial. She gets the firm. Maybe. I'll check. She also gets to do the Palmetto Pointe project solo, if she gets the contract." She became excited. "I bet the county commissioner will give it to Caxton, Chivas & Ross for fear of getting sued for sexual harassment if she doesn't get it! How likely is that?"

Laura shrugged. "Even if she gets it, why would she kill for that? It can't be that huge a commission. It's just another project, and she's already very well-known in her field. To design it on her own is not that much better than designing it with her partners. They'd all get the credit. Mark and Brian seemed to have had the highest opinion of her; they wouldn't have blown off her suggestions."

Kate considered this. "What about personal motives? Maybe she killed them because she hated them. Or, maybe she was having an affair with one of them. The other found out and threatened to make her leave the firm. Or, maybe, she wanted to leave for some other reason, and they wouldn't let her."

"Why wouldn't they let her? Did she have a contract longer than two years? We'll have to find out. And where would she go, to a competitor?" Laura's eyes opened wide. "Hey, maybe she's having an affair with Luke Grimke and deep-sixing her partners was what he wanted."

Kate was agitated. "Wait, we'll get to him in a second. What about opportunity for her? Where was she Saturday morning, at that new home furnishings store, I think, that was having the sale?"

Laura nodded. "Yeah, that's a great store. I almost went by there myself on Saturday, right before I ran into you on King Street. They've got awesome stuff; I got my kitchen lamp there." She pointed at the attractive hand-blown lamp hanging above her computer table. "It's only five minutes from your house; she could've left and come back." Laura nodded sagely, then smiled. "Yes, I could squeeze opportunity out of a rock if I had to."

Kate remained serious. "What about opportunity for Sunday night? Do you know where she was?"

"I heard on Folly Beach, playing with her dog. We'll have to verify that, too." Laura ticked things off on her fingers. "So, again, she has lots of motives and possible opportunity, pending investigation. Who's next?"

Kate nodded. "We're left with Luke Grimke, age fifty-four, born in Palo Alto, California, successful Charleston architect. I've met him a few times. Smooth, sexy, sweet.

Dating a woman a little older than himself. Apparently doesn't go for the babes."

"Nevertheless, what about motive?" Laura considered. "How's his financial situation? I understand he just spent a million dollars on a mansion on Legare Street. And another half a million renovating the place. Maybe he really needed the Palmetto Pointe project. Maybe he was desperate enough to kill for it. Maybe Gigi should watch her back." She thought of Luke's cell phone call in the church; a chill crept up her spine. How did that tie in? She almost shared this with Kate, but decided against it. "What about other motives?"

Kate hypothesized freely. "Jealousy? Betrayal? Having an affair? We don't really know about his personal life, although I'm sure it's interesting. We'll have to find out. And how about opportunity?"

Laura knew about this from the detectives who had visited her on Sunday night. "He was jogging on the Battery when Mark died."

They looked at each other. Kate spoke first. "Okay. That's close. Very close. My house is less than a block from the Battery. People jog through our neighborhood as a shortcut to the Battery all the time."

Silent for a moment, Laura spoke next. "And Sunday night? He wasn't at home. I know because Detective Marcus said they'd gone to see him right before they dropped in on me. Where was he?"

"We'll have to find out." Kate paused, with a thoughtful look on her face.

"Well, let's consider our last suspect," Laura continued. "Cleo Cooper, she's in her early twenties, started working at the firm in July, seems to be doing a good job, but we don't know much else about her. So is it interesting that six weeks after she gets employed, two of her bosses are brutally murdered?"

She immediately regretted her choice of words, but Kate didn't even flinch. Instead, her recently widowed friend answered the rhetorical question in a business-like tone.

"Good question. I would say, absolutely. I'm a scientist and don't put much stock in coincidences. She's kind of a big girl. I know from the two times I've met her, but, even so, I don't think there's much muscle or cunning there. I'd have difficulty imagining her stabbing two people to death." She sighed. "Then again, I have difficulty imagining anyone I know stabbing two people to death! We'll have to find out where she was on Saturday morning and Sunday night. It oughtn't be too difficult to figure out. I think the more interesting question would be whether she heard or saw anything unusual going on in that office." Again Kate hesitated, then got up to get fresh coffee.

She kept talking, her voice carrying easily from the kitchen. "You know, it seems as though everyone's got motives and most of them have opportunity. I thought real life wasn't supposed to be like a mystery novel."

"No, actually, you've got it wrong." Laura accepted a new cup of coffee from her friend, who was almost as comfortable in Laura's new home as Laura was. "Truth is stranger than fiction." She idly flicked on the television, but flicked it off again when she became aware of a snuffling sound. Kate was crying, curled up in a little ball at the far end of the sofa.

"What is it?" Laura couldn't think of anything else to say, but sat down next to her friend, stroking her hair and steeling herself for yet another emotional moment.

"There's something else. It's about me." Kate's voice was muffled. "I'm pregnant. And Mark's not the father."

14

Detective Jeff Marcus was in a bad mood. Three murders in seventy-two hours, and it was his ass on the line if they didn't figure out soon what was going on. He's been a cop for sixteen years and had never seen anything quite like this. They didn't have a single real suspect. Granted, they still had to question everyone, following the discovery of Cleo Cooper's body, but that might not get them any further ahead. Often multiple murders made the investigative waters murkier rather than clearer.

He picked up the Subway sandwich he'd bought at CMC while waiting for the pathologist's reports on Caxton and Chivas to come through and took a bite that engulfed half the sandwich. At least he'd been able to sleep a little before being rudely awakened by Hobbs to go out to Folly to make sure everything was done by the book at Grimke's beach house. Although the nephew, Kyle, was a little too smooth for Marcus' taste, he didn't think the kid had done it. It was too weird to murder someone and then sleep for twelve hours. And the kid had no history of violence. Had been in the clink overnight a couple times for drunk and disorderly, but that wasn't too unusual for a frat boy.

Grimke himself, on the other hand, definitely deserves some further attention, Marcus thought as he finished the sandwich, got a cup of coffee and put his feet up on his desk to scan the two autopsy reports.

Caxton had been dead approximately sixty to ninety minutes when he was discovered at nine o'clock. He had died of a single stab wound just below the thoracic cavity, which had horizontally transected the abdominal aorta.

There were some fragments of aortic wall consistent with deliberate movement of the blade after the initial impact. To Marcus, this translated into someone sticking the knife in there and viciously moving it around to ensure maximum damage. *Jesus.* He read on. Caxton had lost consciousness within half a minute, bleeding out his entire blood volume of over six liters in about two minutes. There was no sign of a struggle, no tissue or fiber under his nails, and no bruises. Interestingly, his hands were unbloodied; it appeared that he had not even pressed his hands to the wound site in a futile attempt to save himself. *Who surprised you so completely?* Marcus wondered.

The second report confirmed what Marcus already knew. The mechanism of death was almost identical to that of the first victim. Aorta horizontally severed "with almost surgical precision." *Hmm, practice makes perfect.* The cut was cleaner this time, with less fragmentation, and the imprint of a knife handle was visible on the victim's abdomen. Time to exsanguinate, also about two minutes. There was some blood found on the victim's hands, but it was difficult to know the significance of this, as the body was supine with hands curled under it, completely soaked in rain when found. Twelve bruised purple irises were also found under and next to the body. Not the killer's bizarre calling card, Marcus knew, but rather a purchase made by the deceased's wife just prior to the her husband's death. *Poor woman.*

Marcus shook his head, then looked up as Hobbs came into their office, bringing along a burst of sound and color from the front offices of the Lockwood Drive police station before quickly closing the door behind him. They had been working together for twelve years; sometimes Marcus thought Hobbs could read his mind.

He did so today. "Woman's crime, you're thinkin'?"

Marcus tossed the reports on his desk. He couldn't explain why stabbing, though it took a certain amount of physical strength, always struck him as a female crime. Maybe it was his old-fashioned upbringing: a woman, in the kitchen, goaded too far, grabs a steak knife, moves in for the kill, heart of stone, nerves of steel. "Woman's crime, but a woman with surgical knowledge."

Hobbs looked at him. "Could be the wife," he acknowledged. "She did a surgical internship before starting on the eye thing. She's got the edge over other suspects so far, I'll say that. No alibi to support her whereabouts between seven forty-five and eight fifty-five on the day in question. She was five minutes from home when Lindross spotted her at eight fifty-five. And her husband probably wouldn't have suspected a thing when she went after him with that blade." He shook his head. The murder weapon had not been recovered. "She says she was walking down King Street, window shopping and getting a cup of coffee, but we've canvassed the entire street. No one remembers her. So, where the hell was she?"

Marcus looked thoughtful. "I hate it when they lie. She should just tell us the truth, so we could get on with it. Any evidence of an affair, either of them, financial problems, anything?"

Hobbs shook his head. "Nah, we should be so lucky! The only interesting thing is on the phone bill from Saturday morning. Bell South finally got us the records. It looks like the deceased made a telephone call to the office at seven-ten; apparently, when there was no answer there, he called his partner, Ross, at home, at seven-twelve. They spoke for less than a minute. Makes me wonder if they had a meeting set up."

"Or a little rendezvous? She's hot stuff all right." Marcus pursed his lips in a silent whistle.

Hobbs made a dismissive gesture. "Or thinks she is. Chivas' wife says they did sometimes meet on Saturday, early, so they could be back with their families by eight. But she wasn't aware of any plans for that particular day."

"But her husband wasn't even in the country," Marcus stated the obvious. "Why would they tell her?"

"Beats the hell out of me, it was just an interesting finding. And Ross's tale of spending the morning shopping actually looks like it's panning out. She was the first customer in the store at seven-thirty and appears to have been there the whole morning, except when she was across the street getting coffee at Starbucks. She's known everywhere, I guess, a true shopaholic."

"Hmm, I don't guess we're any further along than before you walked your ass through the door." Marcus had just gotten the words out when the telephone rang. Hobbs picked up the receiver, but the conversation was short. He grunted once and returned the receiver to the cradle. Marcus raised inquiring eyebrows.

"Looks like our shady lady's got an alibi," he said. "Someone saw Kate Caxton leaving CMC and walking down Ashley Avenue to Calhoun Street at eight o'clock on Saturday morning. They just finished up with the witness, and, apparently, he's reliable. Some visiting professor from Yale. She could never have finished with her patients at seven forty, hurried home, killed her husband and made it back to Ashley Avenue by eight; it's too far."

"Could she have taken a cab?" Marcus wondered. "Stranger things have happened."

Hobbs considered this and decided they should check up on it. "Another way to verify her whereabouts would be to check the dictation system. That's pretty carefully regulated in any major hospital for medico-legal reasons. If she did do a couple dictations on Saturday morning like she said in her statement, we should be able to find them."

Marcus nodded, then spoke slowly, puzzled. "But what about the neighbor, Sullivan, who says he saw her go up the walk at just before seven forty-five? He knows her and also seems reliable."

Hobbs shrugged. "Maybe his clock was wrong, or he got confused and dreamed it, or maybe he has a reason to lie. It makes the most sense that he saw no one go up that walk. If you haven't already, finish up the background search on him; we'll review it. In the meantime, it's looking like Caxton didn't do it. What else have we got?"

Marcus crumpled up his napkin and threw it into the trash can behind his partner's desk without looking. "Nada," he said, accepting a two-point salute from Hobbs. "Let's go check out alibis for last night."

* * * * *

"Well, that was completely and utterly unilluminating," remarked Hobbs as they emerged from the little surf shop on the south side of Market Street where Cleo's boyfriend, Joey Hamilton, worked. Hamilton had displayed no emotion when the policemen had arrived nor had he said much when they took him into the small office in the back of the store to tell him about the unexpected demise of his live-in girlfriend.

"Dude!" Had been his only comment as the story unfolded. He had been at home the entire evening and had two buddies who could vouch for him. He admitted that, on the last night of her life, he and Cleo had argued, and she had said she would be out with a girlfriend. Apparently, this was not an uncommon occurrence for them. Joey had not been worried when she had failed to return home. Detective Marcus forebore to ask whether she routinely turned up in other men's beds, but got the impression that their understanding was of a somewhat loose nature.

The young man appeared either unwilling or unable to provide any insight into the deceased's job or future plans. After he provided them with the name of Cleo's parents in Hoboken, New Jersey, the two detectives took their leave. Their last view of Mr. Hamilton was of him ringing up the price on two lava lamps and a wet suit. He did not watch them leave.

Hobbs decided to drive around the corner to Amanda Michaels' house. After that, they would go further afield to question the two new widows as well as Gigi Ross and Laura Lindross.

Amanda was at home. In an eerie repeat of their visit seventy-two hours before, she invited them in, offered drinks and then settled into her large easy chair. Hobbs thought it was large enough to seat two people easily. He did most of the talking.

"Ms. Michaels, we're here to ask you a couple questions concerning a young lady named Cleo Cooper, a secretary at the architectural firm Caxton, Chivas & Ross."

Amanda looked confused, apparently not sure where Hobbs was going with this.

"Can you tell us where you were between ten o'clock last night and two o'clock this morning?"

"Well, yes, I was right here, at home, asleep. Or trying to fall asleep, I should say. I don't sleep well as it is, and these recent murders have unsettled me a little bit." Recognition dawned. "Oh my God, she's dead too, isn't she?"

Hobbs tried to ask more questions, but Amanda began to cry and seemingly could not stop. "She was quite young, wasn't she?" Amanda shook her head. "No, I never met her, but I think she came into the gallery the other day. Melanie talked to her, about something, I'm not sure what, because I was too far away to hear, but I believe that's how I know the name. Melanie mentioned who she was after she had left. I knew it sounded familiar. And now she's dead, I can't believe it." She blew her nose and fixed Hobbs with a baleful, red-rimmed glance. "Can't you do something about it? Do something!"

The detectives left. Hobbs said nothing until they were back in their squad car. "Why do *I* feel guilty?"

* * * * *

Concomitantly, Gigi, wondering about Melanie's emotional state, called the Chivas home on Tradd Street. Much to her surprise, Melanie answered the telephone. Fifteen minutes later the two women were commiserating in the cozy kitchen. They drank hot peach tea. Domino was nearby.

"Melanie," Gigi's voice was gentle. "You've got to pull yourself together. There's got to be a reason for Brian's death. Not to mention Mark's. You and I together should be able to figure this out. Between the two of us, we knew Brian better than anyone. Did he have some other business venture with Mark that we don't know about? I worry about whether my life is in danger; I find myself looking over my shoulder a good bit, but I really feel like it's related to their relationship, not to the firm, necessarily. I'm now the owner of the firm, but you and Kate get their life interest. I wasn't a full partner yet." She looked at Melanie, who was holding her head in her hands and staring out the window. "I know you must be wondering if I did it."

Melanie looked at Gigi. "I haven't really been worrying about that. I know about the state of Brian's affairs. It seems like the only thing you've gained is an architectural firm with a good reputation. You can keep up the Broad Street offices, but you have to buy out your two partners, or in this case, their wives, before you start keeping all the income for yourself. For Kate and me, it's a pretty good deal. Either we sell and make money, or you work there, and we make money." She sighed. "Believe me, I've considered you the way I've been considering everybody else, but you're not standing out in the crowd."

"Who is?" Gigi was curious.

"Honestly?" Melanie sat still for a moment, then abruptly raised her hands, palms out. "I have no idea."

Gigi sighed. "Me neither," she said, then jumped as her cellular phone rang. She pulled it out of her spacious purse and answered on the third ring. "Hello?"

Melanie got up for more coffee, listening to snatches of conversation. It sounded as if Gigi was speaking to one of the detectives involved with the case. When she finally hung up the telephone, she looked older than her forty-one years.

"That was Detective Hobbs," she said carefully, as if worried that she would burst into tears at any minute. "My secretary, you know, the firm's secretary, Cleo Cooper, was murdered last night."

Melanie's shock was evident on her face. "Oh my God, someone's killing off the whole firm!"

Gigi slumped forward in her chair. The air of authority that made her intimidating to men and women alike was gone. "Melanie, I'm scared." She spoke quietly.

Melanie hastened to reassure her. "Honey, you're safe

as long as you stay around other people. You're more than welcome to stay here if you like. It's a little...empty without, well, you know, at the moment. Truly, I'd love to have you."

Gigi looked stricken. "Oh Melanie, I'm sorry, look at everything you're going through, and I'm panicking about some theoretical risk that probably won't ever come to pass." She hugged the younger woman.

"The police are on their way over and said maybe I can get a ride with them or a squad car to check the house periodically." She looked affectionately at Max, who was lying peacefully at her feet. "And I've got Max to protect me too."

After the officers finished with yet another round of questioning, they left with Gigi in tow, having insisted on twenty-four hour police protection. Melanie sat at the kitchen table.

What the hell had been going on at that firm?

* * * * *

Veronica Parker lived in a sedate home at the west end of St. Michael's Alley. This affluent street, tucked away between Church and Meeting Streets, just south of the bustle of the Broad Street business district, is one of the most picturesque in the historic district. Yellow roses climbed over brick walls, and well-worn marble steps led up to Veronica's heavy oak front door. She did not seem surprised to have company; the reason was obvious as soon as she spoke.

"Come in, gentlemen. I imagine that this is about Mr. Grimke and his whereabouts on Monday evening. He told me you might be stopping by to see me." She smiled, but it seemed to Marcus that the smile did not reach to her eyes. "May I offer some refreshment, or is this strictly business?"

The men declined a drink. Veronica answered their questions with dispatch. She was cool and business-like. Luke had been with her from early evening until approximately midnight, at which time he told her he was heading out to do a little work in his home office before retiring.

"I heard the bells in the steeple of St. Michael's Church striking midnight shortly after he left."

Hobbs strained his neck trying to catch a glimpse of the imposing church just a few dozen feet to the north, beyond a Charleston single house that was reportedly haunted. "I'd imagine those bells are quite loud," he offered benignly. "You're in pretty close proximity to the church, aren't you?"

Veronica smiled and something warm sprang into her eyes. Hobbs wondered if she perhaps liked where the conversation was going. "It's funny," she offered, "most days I don't even hear the bells anymore; I'm so used to them. It's kind of like when you wear your wedding ring for so long that you only feel it when it's off your finger, leaving an empty space. I remember after Hurricane Hugo, back in 1989, the damaged bells were sent to England for repair, and the silence was deafening! It drove us all crazy for a while!" She glanced at the homes of her neighbors and smiled. "I don't know what made me hear them last night. I stayed at home, didn't go out again." She shrugged, then met Hobbs' gaze. "Do you have any other questions?"

"Just one, Ms. Parker," Hobbs hoped she wouldn't take offense. "How long have you been seeing Mr. Grimke?"

"Several months, Detective," Veronica replied. "He's a very sweet man, warm and interesting."

"Thank you for taking the time with us today, ma'am. We appreciate getting answers to our questions."

As Hobbs was leaving, Veronica lifted limpid eyes to his. "Three murders in as many days? It seems to me that you have plenty of questions left to ask, Detective."

* * * * *

Laura stared at Kate in a moment of disbelief. Then, realizing that she was not being a very good friend, she tried to hide her surprise behind a sympathetic exterior.

"I knew you weren't telling me everything," she chided gently. "Maybe this will add a piece to the puzzle."

It was the wrong thing to say.

"I don't see how!" Kate responded. "Mark knew nothing of all this; the baby's father doesn't know yet either. I only found out myself on Friday night." She stopped. Her confusion was mirrored on Laura's face.

"You found out that you're pregnant on Friday night, and the next morning your husband is killed?" Laura said. "These are two major events that I can't believe are not connected!"

Kate shook her head. "I'm telling you, nobody knew. It was a drugstore pregnancy test that I did quickly at home. It's not like the results are on the CMC computer or on our answering machine! I'm telling you, Laura, Mark couldn't have seen the results anywhere!"

Laura looked thoughtful. "Are you sure the baby's father didn't know? How badly did he want you to leave Mark?" She turned to face her friend. "Kate, this is huge. You've got to tell me everything. And you can start by telling me who the baby's father is."

15

hat evening, Kate, exhausted by the events of the
day, finished a cup of tea and realized her self-con-
trol was at an end. The police had thoroughly questioned her about the third death at Laura's Fort Sumter
House flat that afternoon.

"My whereabouts? Last night?" She was tired of all the
questions. "I finished up at work around eight o'clock and
got Melanie Chivas discharged from the hospital. We had
dinner at Pusser's Landing, had gone there to discuss our
husbands' funeral plans, if you must know. I dropped her
off at her house at about nine-thirty. We were both exhausted; she insisted on spending the night alone. I thought
it was a bit early for her to be all by herself, but she wanted
it that way, so I told her I'd be on my cell phone if she
needed me and went straight home. I fell asleep in one of
my big armchairs sometime after that."

"Did you receive any telephone calls last night?"

"Yes, actually, the phone rang once, but I let the machine pick it up. I wasn't in the mood to talk. And no one
left a message." Her opaque gaze said she wasn't wanting
to talk now, either.

The police asked similar questions of Laura before they
left, and Laura had walked Kate downstairs shortly after
that.

"Don't let them get you down, Kate. You've had some
huge life events happen to you in the last few days. Thank
you for sharing this most recent one with me. I'm so happy
for you! I won't breathe a word. You go home and rest.
Remember what Lord Peter Wimsey always said?" She
looked at her friend inquiringly, clearly concerned that their

friendship might be doomed if Kate had not read any Dorothy L. Sayers.

Kate, however, nodded, and Laura continued. "He said 'Trouble shared is trouble halved.' Everything's going to turn out fine."

Now at home on Lamont Street, Kate couldn't stand it anymore. Her exhaustion, both physical and emotional, was complete. She reached for the telephone and dialed. When the other end was picked up, a smile lit her face.

"Hi, ...I'm fine, but I miss you. Can I come over?"

Receiving an affirmative answer, Kate, her spirits buoyed immeasurably, hurried to put on a pair of boots and her leather jacket, bought while she was a pretty, carefree college student on her junior year in Paris. She grabbed her shoulder bag and hurried outside.

She saw no one as she ran over to the car and started the engine.

Her destination was just a few blocks away, on the west side of King Street, next to the graveyard associated with the Unitarian Church on Archdale Street. She found a parking spot with little difficulty and entered the secluded gate, stepping quietly on the slate pathway that led into the depths of the cemetery. A few steps down the path, on her right, there were several old wrought iron gates, leading in sequentially to a series of different apartments all in the same sprawling building. It had received numerous additions over the decades, and an atmosphere of benign neglect now hung over the place. It had the settled, calm feeling of the New Orleans French Quarter after a successful Mardi Gras, with black wrought iron detail, green ferns hanging from the balconies, the scent of coffee and old perfume, and the faint sound of jazz drifting over the summer night from someone's carelessly adjusted radio.

Feeling like twenty again, Kate's heart filled with anticipation as she went through the last gate and across the deserted courtyard to the rickety staircase hugging the southern side of the house. On the top floor, she stopped in front of a screen door. Knocking gently, her heart lit as she saw Jimmy coming toward her.

He was tall and rangy, a boy, really, Kate thought with a pang, wearing jeans that hung low on his narrow hips. His chest was bare; a trail of fur led from his navel downwards to an area she had previously explored and would soon encounter again. He was barefoot, and his blond hair was lit from behind by the light of the golden kitchen. A red dish towel was flung over one shoulder. There was a smudge of spaghetti sauce on one cheek. His sea-colored eyes, half green and half blue, smiled at her as he held open the screen door. He planted a kiss on her lips before reaching past her to close the door and push her toward the kitchen.

He was nineteen years old, and she was in love with him.

The first day she had seen him, as she was walking home from work, and he was returning from an afternoon class at College of Charleston, she had known they would have a history. The concept of him became the simplest thing in her life and the most complex. She had seen him twice more before he said hello. He had invited her up to his apartment after they had stood talking in the street for a few minutes. There had been no pretense in his invitation. He had known what she wanted. They had barely entered the apartment before his mouth was warm on hers. His hands explored her body as if he had a right to be there, and, as he unzipped her skirt, she was impressed at his un-self-conscious need. Their togetherness was so obvious and natural to him that afterward she had lain in his arms, utterly content, feeling as if she had known his serene spirit forever.

He had dated in high school, but had none of the emotional baggage that defined every adult relationship in which she had previously participated. He was sweet and sexy enough to have the experience of a much older man, but young enough to know that life was still pure and promising. They saw each other as often as possible. He gave himself to her completely and was unlike anyone she had ever known.

Later, she told him of her marriage, her career, and her age, and he accepted this information as a part of her world. He seemed to know that eventually she would do the right thing.

Jimmy followed her into the kitchen, where a bottle of red wine was open and glasses were waiting. They had not seen each other since the morning of her husband's death.

"Jimmy," her voice was as soft as his fingers on her bare stomach. "I had to come over, I was going crazy, not seeing you. The whole thing with Mark has been so hard. I can't even pretend I care; my friends all think I'm hard and unfeeling, but it's just not relevant. All that matters is being with you."

"I know, baby, you don't have to explain," he was scorching her skin with his hands, and she was having difficulty breathing. "I've missed you too."

He drew away. She watched him step out of his jeans and come toward her. No one had ever given her as much pleasure as this uncomplicated boy. She would do anything to be with him, her soul mate, her southern boy, her best friend.

The conversation was complete.

Afterward, they danced on the small balcony to old favorites that played on the radio. He wore faded boxers, and she was in his gray flannel bathrobe. He teased her for remembering when some of the songs had first come out. They fed each other spaghetti that he had made and they had warmed in the microwave. The cemetery below added an otherworldly serenity; the headstones reflected the pale moonlight. It was the first time since Mark's death that she felt utterly at peace. She had done the right thing.

It was after nine o'clock when Kate left Jimmy's apartment. She was completely unprepared to meet anyone in the street and was particularly distressed to see Detectives Hobbs and Marcus loitering next to her car, their squad car parked a short distance away. She had no choice but to approach and greet them, gritting her teeth in their presence for the second time that day.

"Good evening, gentlemen. What can I do for you?" She was quite sure that a calm demeanor would not help her this time.

"Visiting a friend, Dr. Caxton?" Marcus' voice was like butter over hot rum. Kate knew a trap when she heard one.

"Yes, indeed, officer." *Never apologize, never explain.*

"At nine o'clock at night?"

Kate raised her eyebrows and nodded, smiling slightly, as if the question were merely conversational and a bit irrelevant, a question about the weather on an obviously sunny day.

The police officers looked at each other. Hobbs nodded.

Just as they were preparing to move away, Jimmy came through the arched gateway, his bare feet making little slapping noises on the gray slate. He was wearing his faded blue jeans and nothing else. Sculpted pectoralis muscles were hard to miss even in the dark. His tawny hair was rumpled, and, even though Kate knew she was in trouble, her heart still missed a beat just looking at him. In his hands he held a silky undergarment.

He opened his mouth, but saw the policemen before any words came out. Hobbs advanced, and Jimmy recovered his speech, calmly stuffing the brassiere into his pocket.

"What's going on, officer?" He sounded concerned, but not overly so. Kate saw the questions in his eyes, however, and knew Marcus would pick up on this as well. "Is the young lady okay?"

Marcus looked from him to Kate. "Dr. Caxton, do you know this gentleman?"

Keenly aware of her responsibilities as a physician and her need to have ethics above reproach in the community, Kate slowly nodded her head.

* * * * *

When Laura's telephone rang, she knew something bad had happened. She listened to Kate telling her about Jimmy's arrest. Despite the fact that she had a reasonable suspicion of Jimmy's guilt, Laura listened to her friend.

"They don't believe me when I say we were together on Saturday morning. They think Jimmy killed Mark. I know he didn't do it! He was fast asleep when I got there at eight o'clock. And on Sunday night he was at home, but no one can support that, so they're saying he went to the Harris Teeter in the pouring rain and knifed a guy he didn't even know in a split second in a public parking lot! Laura, why would he kill Brian? He had no motive! And now this Cleo Cooper thing is making him look really bad because he said he was on Folly last night with his buddy, who has a house there. He admitted all that before even knowing about Cleo. Laura, I believe him. I know he couldn't have done this. What should I do?"

Listening to the hysteria in her friend's voice, Laura shed her pale blue cotton nightgown and slipped into jeans and a turtleneck. Adding her boots, she found her car keys and was already at the door when Kate pathetically said: "Can you come get me? He's being held without bail."

"Honey, there's nothing else you can do. I'll be right there." And, for the second time that day, she added: "Don't worry, everything's going to be fine."

16

L aura collected a hysterical Kate from the police station. She brought her home to Lamont Street and, after hot tea and talk, tucked her in bed, then sat in the living room of the house of the first murdered man while she considered the crimes.

She felt she was at a crossroads. She could help her friend, her only real friend in Charleston, or she could sit back and let the police sort things out. She decided to operate on the assumption that everything Kate told her was true. In that case, Kate was guilty of adultery with a much younger man. She had gotten pregnant by him and discovered this on Friday evening. She had told no one, going about her evening as usual, getting up early the next morning for work, leaving with her coffee at seven o'clock. She had finished at work before eight, left CMC and walked downtown to King Street where she had stolen an hour with her lover, leaving his apartment only seconds before Laura saw her and gave her a ride home. She had not gotten coffee on King Street nor had she window-shopped. She had not entered the Lamont Street home at seven forty-five as Bill Sullivan had claimed. Who had he seen? Had he seen anyone? Or did he have a reason to lie?

Laura decided to pay Bill Sullivan a visit. She looked across the street. It was late, but his lights were still on. Leaving Kate in her bed, Laura seized the moment.

* * * * *

"Of course I saw her." Bill seemed a little miffed at her line of inquiry. He took a deep breath and blew it out, eyeing his visitor suspiciously. "Why would I lie? I barely knew what was going on over there when the police came to question me."

"I'm not questioning your veracity, Mr. Sullivan," Laura said, although she was. "But did you maybe get the time wrong or, uh, dream her up?"

Sullivan frowned for a moment, then laughed. "You've got a hell of a nerve, coming in here and asking me all these questions. But I understand. You don't think your friend did it. Well, I'm here to tell you that I don't think she did it either. I like the doctor. She's real friendly. And she always asks about the dogs. But I know what I saw, and you're gonna have to account for that in your little scenario of what happened Saturday morning. She went right up the walk, red hair, black turtleneck, khaki pants, didn't pause for a second, turned that doorknob and entered the house like she owned it. I can't tell you otherwise because that's what happened, and that's the God's truth."

* * * * *

Back in Fort Sumter House, Laura was more confused than ever. Assuming Sullivan's story was valid, she decided she was left with a single alternative. Someone dressed up as Kate Caxton had entered the house, killed her husband and gotten clean away. Who could it have been?

She considered carefully. It was more than likely a woman. She doubted that Bill Sullivan's practiced eye would have been taken in by a man in drag. So Luke Grimke was out and Jimmy, too. For the moment, anyway. That left Amanda, Gigi, and Melanie. And possibly Cleo, because maybe someone murdered the murderer. The last murder had a different modus operandi, after all—strangulation, the officers had explained. Was there anyone else? Luke's girlfriend, perhaps? Did Mark have a girlfriend no one knew about? Kate had suspected this, but was too happy with Jimmy to care. Where could he have met her? Had he taken any recent business trips? Could it really have been Amanda?

Amanda. Laura considered her. She had adored Mark, agreed to marry him. Apparently she hadn't dated since they broke up, years ago. She was obviously devastated by his death, pale as a ghost, losing weight, avoiding her friends. Was this someone wracked with guilt? Laura sighed. And the girl had plenty of opportunity. Late to the gallery on Saturday, at the Harris Teeter on Sunday night, for God's sake, and no alibi for Monday night either. Yes, it could be Amanda. The only problem was her weak motive for killing Brian and Cleo. Had they found out about the affair and had to be silenced? Laura could think of no other motives, but she put Amanda high on her list. With a red wig, her slender frame could easily have been mistaken for Kate's.

And, speaking of redheads, what about Gigi? A woman of a certain age, working with two powerful men, loving them, hating them, jealous of them? She was the last person to whom Mark had spoken before he died. Why had he telephoned her? Maybe to pass along vital information that subsequently cost him and Brian their lives? Why had Gigi not mentioned the telephone call? Was Gigi methodically destroying the firm so she could have it for herself? Laura found it hard to believe that someone could kill three people, all of whom worked with her, and think she would not be caught. But, she reflected, Gigi was as bold as anyone she knew, and maybe her alibis were too convenient. Or was she next on the killer's list?

How about Melanie? A good person, Laura felt, in a happy marriage. What had she uncovered about her husband and his business partner that would have made her want to kill them? Laura couldn't think of a thing, except possibly adultery, and, even then, she had difficulty imagining Melanie flying into a rage over anything. It was also hard to imagine her cold-bloodedly donning a red wig and setting out for the Lamont Street home. Undeniably, though, her opportunities were there. She had no alibi for the gallery Saturday morning, nor for Monday night. And she had undoubtedly been present at the scene of the crime on Sunday night. But for her to kill her own husband... Laura shivered. She could not imagine it.

And how was Cleo involved? *Cleo's the key in all this*, she decided. What had the secretary known? *It has to be related to the office*, Laura thought.

Laura sighed. Whether she liked it or not, these were her main suspects. She would have to ask difficult questions of everyone involved.

I'll start in the morning, first thing, she decided. *In the meantime, let's see what I can find out about this cast of characters on the Internet.*

She poured a cup of coffee and, not feeling the least bit sleepy, turned on her computer.

* * * * *

Gigi awoke on Wednesday morning in a panic, thinking she was late for work. Then she remembered the events of the preceding days. She got up and walked to the drawing room, to the windows looking out onto Wentworth Street. The police car ostentatiously parked out front did not comfort her. Hearing Max behind her, wanting his walk, she pulled on her sweat shirt and adjusted the black hood around her neck.

Even in South Carolina, autumn mornings could be chilly.

* * * * *

Laura awoke early on Wednesday morning as well, after a short, dreamless sleep. She pulled on her favorite bathrobe and went into the kitchen, taking in the view from the French windows as she crossed the living room. It was newly light; a faint blush of pink and gold adorned the southwestern horizon. The Connector was visible, too, as a faint gray ribbon above the Ashley River, iridescent in the early morning haze. After pouring a cup of coffee, Laura went out onto the balcony and sat in the cool of the morning, the breeze playing at the hem of her robe, sending a momentary chill up her legs.

Her computer search last night had been interesting. At least one person was hiding something. *Something pretty big*, Laura's mouth curved in a smile. She enjoyed traveling and a trip out to San Francisco was always fun. She would leave late in the afternoon. But, first, there were people to see.

An hour later, she was on her way to the Michaels & Moore Gallery. It was closed, so she walked one block over to State Street, reflecting again on how close Amanda lived to her gallery. A one-minute walk brought her to the small pink cottage that Amanda called home. It was eight-fifteen, not too early to pay a sympathetic call on a friend. *Well, an acquaintance, anyway*, Laura thought as she rang the glowing bell.

The door, made of dark, polished wood, was opened so

promptly that Laura almost had the sense Amanda had been waiting for her. She was pale, with her pinky-blonde hair framing saucer-like brown eyes. Her pale pink sweat suit served only to emphasize her albino appearance. Her eyes were sad, but Laura could have sworn that she had recently applied lipstick.

"Oh, Laura, come in, how nice of you to come by; I was just wishing for some company. Would you like tea?" She indicated the mug she was holding. Laura, feeling a moment of alertness in her brain, accepted. She suddenly remembered someone telling her that Amanda did not drink coffee. For some reason, she thought of the oversized coffee cup in the Caxton kitchen on the morning of the murder. Had Mark been expecting Amanda that morning, forgetting after all the years, that she didn't drink coffee? Preceding her guest into the kitchen, Amanda reached for a tea bag and dropped it into a mug, immediately drowning it in hot water from a kettle on the gas stove. She offered sugar and milk, both of which Laura declined.

The women settled in the living room, Laura on the comfortably squishy leather sofa, and Amanda in her deep, oversized armchair, with a blanket and well-worn velvet pillows surrounding her.

"Amanda, I wanted to see how you're doing," Laura began, thinking Amanda actually seemed happy to see her.

"I'm fine," Amanda said. "I admit I wasn't at first, because Mark was once such a big part of my life, but things are better now. I'll be getting back to work next week, and they do say that time heals all wounds."

"Why does Mark's death bother you so much?"

Amanda gazed at Laura over the rim of her mug, her brown eyes as large as a little girl's. "Have you ever had someone you love, really love, die?" She asked soberly.

Laura thought about it. She never had. Her parents were very much alive, recently retired to the island of St. Croix. Her siblings were healthy. Her ex-boyfriends were happily pursuing life, some more happily than she cared to admit. Even her man of the moment, an editor for Doubleday, had just called her that morning from New York City to postpone his next visit.

"No, I haven't."

Amanda tried to explain her sense of loss for something that had meant too much for too long and was now never to be.

"Were you angry enough to want to see him suffer when he left you?"

Amanda considered, not seeming affronted by the question. "Truthfully?" She cocked her head to the side, birdlike, her eyes bright with remembered emotion. "Yes, I suppose I was. He left me, with little explanation and no apology, for someone else, after leading me to believe we'd be married that autumn. I was livid. He made me look like a fool. I didn't want everyone's sympathy. I wanted revenge. It's really only been in the last year that I've realized that indifference is the best revenge. I didn't care how he was doing. I stopped thinking about him every damn day, and I quit worrying that I'd run into him in the grocery store or on the street."

Laura spoke carefully. "Speaking of grocery stores, what brought you to the Harris Teeter on Sunday night? I'm sure the police have already suggested to you that it's quite a coincidence."

Amanda shook her head. "No one's suggested anything," she said. "They've been very kind. I was there because Melanie had mentioned it at work; I realized I needed to pick up a few things, too. I finished at the gallery at nine o'clock and drove over after that." Her eyes met Laura's. "I didn't kill Brian, if that's what you're getting at. It's true I was late to the gallery on Saturday, but I was here asleep, not South of Broad killing Mark. I'm about as unathletic as I look, Laura." She raised pale, skinny arms. "I don't have the strength to stick a knife into a turkey at Thanksgiving, let alone into big, strong men." She sounded as if her thoughts had traveled along this route before.

Laura watched her quarry closely. "Have you heard about Cleo Cooper, the Caxton, Chivas & Ross secretary?" She asked gently, but Amanda was already nodding.

"Yes, I have, it's horrible. The poor girl, she was only twenty-three, just starting her life. The police came over yesterday afternoon to talk to me. It sounds like Luke Grimke is being questioned pretty closely. I guess she was strangled at his beach house, and he was alone on Monday night."

Laura felt the early glow of satisfaction for a job well done. *I guess Luke has more than one thing to hide.* She noticed Amanda's half-closed eyes; it was as if she were speaking from a memorized script.

"Were you with anyone on Monday night?" Laura asked as casually as she could.

Amanda's voice was soft. "No one."

Laura left the cottage with the distinct impression that Amanda was on something. Maybe sedatives or pain killers, or possibly just exhausted.

She wandered north up State Street to the Market and then over to King Street. She intended to do a bit of shopping at the new Metropolitan Store on the west side of King Street before looping back to Ansonborough to drop in on Gigi Ross.

Laura entered the double-wide doors of the store that

had opened in Charleston only recently, but already had a loyal following. She needed a standing lamp for her bedroom and was also hoping that a sales clerk would remember Gigi's presence there the previous Saturday. Slowly, she set about ingratiating herself with a talkative salesgirl, who seemed only too willing to talk about the murders, in between showing her several handsome lamps.

"It was Theresa the cops asked about the Ross woman. She's in here all the time; that day wasn't any exception. She was the first customer through the door, as I heard her say. That was at seven-thirty. She stayed the whole morning, practically, except when she was across the street getting coffee." The girl pointed to the Starbucks, clearly visible through the large side windows. "She loves their mochaccino; Theresa always has to tell her to be careful with the whipped cream, 'cause it drips on the floor. But, to be fair, she bought a pile of stuff by the time she left at ten-thirty. It was so much we had one of the drivers deliver it for her the same day." Laura stopped listening to the squeaky voice as she considered Gigi's alibi. She could have come to the store, slipped out, run over to Lamont Street, murdered Mark, run back, gotten coffee at Starbucks and returned to the Metropolitan Store, with no one the wiser.

"What was Ms. Ross wearing on Saturday?" Laura asked the question abruptly, unaware of how odd it sounded until she saw the salesgirl's puzzled look.

"Wearing? I don't know, you'd have to ask Theresa. She's only here on weekends. But Ms. Ross did buy a gorgeous silk robe in a purple shade that went perfect with her hair."

"Would you have Theresa call me when you talk to her next? I'd really appreciate it." Laura gave the girl her telephone number, feeling like the gumshoe she so often wrote about.

Ten minutes later, she was the proud owner of a new lamp, which she asked to have delivered to her. She also acquired a cup of coffee at Starbucks, where a good-looking young man confirmed Gigi's presence on Saturday morning at the coffee bar. He thought she'd been there at about seven-thirty and again just before nine. *That's odd.* Laura herself had been at Starbucks then and didn't remember seeing Gigi.

Later, sitting in Gigi's rather ornate living room on Wentworth Street, Laura noted that she could very nearly see the parking lot of the Harris Teeter when she looked out the drawing room windows. Gigi had seemed unsurprised to see her. Laura wondered for a moment if Amanda had alerted her.

"What can I do for you?" She inquired after offering coffee, which Laura declined.

Laura took a deep breath. "Gigi, I've been thinking about who might be responsible for the deaths of your partners and secretary. It might be you."

Gigi's eyes did not move from Laura's face. Then she flung back her head and laughed. Her hair ran in a sunlit cascade down her back, its deeper hues finding a reflection in the red of the drawing room walls. She looked at Laura with a mischievous smile playing around her lips.

"What are you, the master sleuth who, in the final chapters, pulls everything together for the startling denouement?" She wiped her eyes. "Go on, let's brainstorm. Tell me how I masterminded this triumvirate of killings."

Laura smiled, despite herself. She liked this woman. "Okay, I don't know that it was you. I just wanted your reaction," she admitted. "I do have it narrowed down; you're in there, but that's all I have."

Guided by Laura's questions, Gigi described her alibis. "Saturday morning I was downtown shopping. I got home around eleven o'clock and saw the news of Mark's death on TV. I was at Metropolitan the whole morning, except when I went to get coffee across the street. Then, on Sunday, when Brian died, I was on Folly Beach with Max. The police already went over all this with me. We saw people out on the beach; two people, I guess, came forward on my behalf as witnesses. They remembered seeing a woman with a big white dog. So that helps me." Gigi smiled. "And on Monday night, I was out of town. From what I gather, Cleo was killed between ten and midnight when I was on Hilton Head."

"Anyone see you out there?" Laura felt that her question was routine and was surprised at the response it drew from Gigi. Her face lost its animation and confidence; she suddenly looked to be near tears.

"If it were very important, I could probably muster one up," she said. "Thank God, no one's asked me yet." She took a deep breath, and the Jack Citron story came spilling out. "I don't know what I keep expecting," she finished, getting up to paw through her purse, "but it sure isn't pre-dawn drives to my own cold bed, feeling like a cheap whore." Her eyes were filled with tears as she handed Laura Jack's business card. "Laura, please don't tell anyone," she begged. "I'll tell the police if I have to, but I think they might let it go."

Laura gave her word and consoled the distraught woman. Then she was left with just one last question. "Gigi, why did Mark call you at home on Saturday morning?"

The older woman did not answer for a moment. "I don't know," she finally said. "And that will bother me for the rest of my life. He said he had to talk to me immediately about something. Then, in the next breath, he said that there was someone at the door; he would call me back. I told him I'd be on my cell phone—he caught me just as I was heading out—and he hung up without saying good-bye." She looked thoughtful. "That was the last time I heard from him." She looked soberly at Laura. "I think that whoever was at the door came to kill him."

Laura was silent, adding this next piece to the jigsaw puzzle. It fit. Someone came to see Mark at seven-fifteen, someone who had perhaps seen his wife leave fifteen minutes before. They talked, argued, and, a few minutes later, Mark was dead.

Who had it been?

17

L aura drove to Charleston Medical Center next. She parked in visitor parking and made her way to the Department of Ophthalmology. The waiting room was a hushed space of dark wood and cappuccino-colored walls, not unlike the color scheme in her own apartment. A receptionist wearing a small headset was ensconced at a half-moon shaped desk, elevated on a platform. A coffee machine was set up in one corner. Numerous magazines—*Town & Country, Harper's Bazaar, GQ*—reflected the interests of the mostly wealthy clientele that came to the clinic.

Laura passed the waiting room and made her way down the carpeted hallway to Kate's office. An occasional open examination room door revealed a patient waiting for the white-coated doctor, but mostly the doors were shut and occasionally the murmur of conversation was heard.

Tricia was not in her office, so Laura walked through the secretarial space and stuck her head into Kate's office, knowing that Wednesday was her operating room day and hoping that perhaps she was between cases. She was rewarded by the sight of her friend at her desk, going over some ocular condition with a white-coated resident. Both doctors were in scrubs and appeared to have just come from the OR. Kate saw Laura right away over the top of the resident's head, held up a hand, palm out, in a brief gesture of recognition and continued talking.

"So the scleral buckle supports the vitreous base. Ninety-five percent of all rhegmatogenous retinal detachments are caused by posterior vitreous separation. You know that because of the horseshoe-shaped nature of a retinal break. The gentleman whose surgery we did today had a single horseshoe tear infero-temporally just anterior to the equator. We're supporting the tear on the buckle, but also the rest of the vitreous base for three hundred and sixty degrees. He shouldn't have any further problems."

Laura sat at Tricia's desk until the resident left several minutes later, apparently well-armed in the retinal detachment arena. "I'll dictate the op note," Kate called after him, then turned to Laura.

"Hi, what's up?" She motioned Laura into a chair and flopped into her own black leather chair.

Kate's office was small, but one side was all windows with a view of Charleston rooftops. The cream-colored walls were hung with black-framed diplomas. Two standing lamps emphasized the calm setting. These were on, but the harsh fluorescent ceiling lights were not.

"Done with surgery already?" Laura asked. It was mid-morning. Usually Kate did three or four cases and was done by three-thirty or so.

"Yup, first one was a poorly-controlled diabetic with traction macular detachment. Monocular. I really wanted to avoid iatrogenic breaks. It went well from that point of view, actually. This second case was a tourist from Vermont. Of all the luck, huh?" She seemed unconcerned. "Still, it could be worse. I have to see him tomorrow, then he can fly back. It was an inferior break, so I drained him and didn't use gas. Nothing's going to expand inside his eye as the airplane climbs to thirty thousand feet." She broke off, smiling sheepishly. "Sorry to get technical, let's talk about you."

Laura took her at her word. "I was wondering if you wanted to come downtown with me and have lunch with Melanie. I've talked to Amanda and Gigi about motives and opportunity, but somehow it's hardest of all with Melanie."

Kate smiled. She looked much calmer than she had the night before. "So you've ruled me out, huh?" Her tone turned serious. "Thank you so much for helping me, especially last night. I know Jimmy didn't do it. And we'll figure it out. Let's go see Melanie right now. I'm basically all wrapped up here."

They left the office. "I'm on my pager, if you need me," Kate informed Tricia, who had materialized at her desk, as they walked out.

"No problem, Dr. Caxton," her secretary returned. "Have a nice lunch."

* * * * *

Gigi put down her book and stretched. Although she was trying to enjoy her self-imposed vacation, she knew herself well enough to realize that she was a woman of action and would have difficulty sitting around for the better part of a week. Even Max could only be taken for so many walks. *I would rather have too much to do than too little*, she often told colleagues. The same could be said for her personal life.

After taking a shower in her green and gold bathroom, Gigi dried her hair and got dressed. Sitting at her vanity table in the little annex off the bathroom, she considered her look for the day. She could pull her hair back in a chignon and use false eyelashes to glamorize the severe look. She could leave her hair loose and down play her makeup for a natural look. Or maybe she could go for flirty and playful in a ponytail with one of the new metallic lipsticks she had bought on Hilton Head.

Hilton Head. Gigi frowned, not wanting to remember Jack Citron. After a moment, she shook her head and inspected her face in the mirror. She had good skin, no visible pores, beautiful eyebrows, and a mouth meant for lipstick. Her age was beginning to show, though, especially around her eyes, from years of eyeliner and powder. Maybe she should consider plastic surgery or that new "featherlight" carbon dioxide laser she'd seen advertised on television. *You can't stop the clock*, a little voice inside her head whispered.

Abruptly, Gigi shook her thick wavy hair around her face, added a swipe of nude lipstick and called Max. He came bounding over to her from another part of the house, his tongue hanging out of his mouth, looking at her with sparkling eyes. Gigi felt her insides uncurl. He loved her, no matter what. He didn't care that she wore no foundation, or that her eyes were unadorned. She smiled and played with the ruff of fur around his neck. Then, grabbing her sunglasses, she left the house, the large white dog excitedly straining on the leash.

Thirty minutes later, Gigi felt much better. She had visited Ann Taylor and Nicole Miller, easily spending the five thousand dollars she hadn't dipped into on Hilton Head. *I was born to shop*, she thought happily, as she settled in at Starbucks for a non-fat latte and a pannini sandwich. She loved their new lunch menu. Securing a copy of *The Post & Courier* that had been abandoned at the next table, she settled down to read, occasionally glancing up to make sure Max was behaving himself outside.

Jumping a little as her cellular phone rang inside her handbag, Gigi found the phone and flipped it open. "Gigi Ross," she announced, loving the sound of her name, playful yet sophisticated all at once, she thought. When she got married she would certainly never switch her name.

"Gigi? Luke Grimke here. How are you doing?" His deep voice came pleasantly into her ear.

Gigi Grimke. Nah, not better. "Why, Luke, how nice to hear from you. How are you doing?"

"Well, I'm fine, and I was hoping you are too. I called your office earlier, but I guess you've closed it for the week? Quite right, too, sign of respect for the family, uh, families, and all that." Gigi listened, wondering when he would get to the point. Her insides had started churning again.

"Would you like to have lunch? I have a couple things I wanted to talk to you about," he sounded uncertain, and Gigi smiled despite herself.

"Of course, I'd love to. I need all the moral support I can get!" She gave a little laugh. "I'm actually at Starbucks right now, so I'll just sit tight."

"Great, I'll be right there," Luke sounded relieved.

He was as good as his word and showed up ten minutes later on foot. Gigi remembered that his office was just five blocks away on the western side of Meeting Street. Despite the growing warmth of the day, he looked cool and relaxed in a crisp white shirt and khakis. A dark red tie completed the outfit. *In case he has to go on TV*, Gigi thought. He took off his navy blazer and gave Gigi a quick peck on the cheek before settling into an aluminum and rattan chair opposite her and signalling for a menu.

"You got started without me, I see," he smiled, teasing her.

"What can I say?" Gigi returned, keeping the conversation light. "You got here just in time."

Luke's blue eyes watched her appraisingly, and he was suddenly serious. "Gigi, I'm here for a specific reason. I've been getting a lot of heat from the police since the girl was murdered. I need your help. I know Kyle didn't do it. Is there anything you can tell me that might shed some light on this unfortunate situation? You knew the office politics better than anyone. And you probably knew Mark and Brian better than anyone. You might even know some stuff they'd never tell their wives. Is there anything at all that might help us out?" He shoved a distracted hand through his salt and pepper hair and looked at her imploringly. "I'm really desperate here."

Gigi sighed and looked out the window before glancing over at him again. "I'm not sure what I can do to help, Luke."

"Well, there are other things the police don't know about," Luke confessed. His eyes locked on hers. "We need to talk."

Gigi could not quite read the expression in his eyes.

* * * * *

On the way to the parking lot, Laura told Kate about her upcoming trip to California. They took Laura's car since Kate had walked that morning. She looked pale, as though she hadn't slept much, and Laura reflected that this was probably the case. As the women approached Tradd Street, Laura wondered how Melanie was doing.

Kate's thoughts had apparently wandered in a similar direction. "I wonder how she's holding up. You know, she's pretty tough, but he was the love of her life."

They parked in front of Melanie's house, near Bedon's Alley. The picturesque row houses sat bathed in sunlight, flowers everywhere, and the occasional cat was luxuriating on a narrow section of warm pavement. They rang the bell and, receiving no answer, went around to the unlocked side gate on the eastern side of the property. Melanie liked to spend time in her walled, Italian-style garden.

Melanie was in the garden, reclining on a deck chair with wide-rimmed straw hat and sunglasses on. Domino lay next to her, and she slowly stroked his fur. Her head moved a little as Kate and Laura came through the archway. Laura knew that, under the sunglasses, her eyes were open. She had seen them.

"Good morning, girls," she said. "Thanks so much for coming by." She offered them unsweetened iced tea, adding a sprig of mint to each big glass. They sipped appreciatively as the day was rapidly becoming warm.

Domino, whose allegiance lay solely with Melanie, sought refuge behind a distant rosebush.

"So, what's going on?" Melanie then asked.

There was no easy way to start, so Kate told Melanie about her affair with Jimmy. Both Kate and Laura were startled by Melanie's anger.

"He left a perfectly good woman who loved him to be with you, and you betrayed him!" She spat in Kate's direction. "And now he's dead!" Tears sprang into her eyes. "Maybe it's better that way! He would have been devastated, Kate! What else has been going on? I bet the police will find this turn of events fascinating!"

It took more than twenty minutes before Laura and Kate succeeded in calming their friend down enough to listen to the theory that Mark had also been unfaithful. "Things just weren't the same anymore," Kate explained. "We never talked; he became so distant. It was like we lived completely separate lives. I turned to someone else. I think he was having an affair as well."

Melanie could only shake her head in disbelief and disapproval. "It couldn't have been Amanda, if that's what you're getting at." Melanie was emphatic. "I see Amanda every day. I'd know if she were hiding something. There was no one important in her life." She shook her head. "It had to have been someone else."

Laura told her of the mystery guest who had interrupted Mark's telephone call on Saturday morning, but Melanie seemed only slightly mollified. Reluctantly, Laura persisted. "Why was Amanda late to the gallery that day?"

Melanie shook her head. "She said she overslept, but she never oversleeps, and she only came in at five minutes of eight. I was there for nearly an hour, just answering e-mails and sending bills, until she showed up. I don't know where she was, but I doubt she was down on Lamont murdering Mark." Her eyes flashed. Laura realized Melanie's anger was rooted in Kate's affair. Maybe this was a woman who could kill her philandering husband in a jealous rage.

"Have you heard about the firm's secretary yet?" Kate changed the subject and received a nod from Melanie.

"The police came by yesterday to tell me and ask questions." She shrugged. "Luckily, I have an alibi. I was on the telephone for over two hours on Monday night talking with Brian's brother and sister-in-law about the funeral and the status of the police investigation. We hung up after midnight. They live in San Francisco," she added in explanation. Taking off her sunglasses, Melanie looked at her friends with red-rimmed eyes. "You guys can't possibly think I had anything to do with this!"

"No, of course not, honey," Kate assured her. "We're just trying to make sense of this, trying to figure it out, that's all." She and Laura exchanged weary glances, unwilling to pursue any further questioning.

Conversation moved on to the somber, yet less inflammatory, subject of Brian's funeral, which would also take place at St. Philip's. It was planned for the next afternoon.

* * * * *

Laura gazed at the Pacific Ocean. The flight from Atlanta to San Francisco was not full; she had slept a little, comfortable despite flying economy class. She awoke as they were flying over the Rockies; these had taken her breath away, as they always did. Gradually, the stark granite with the snowy peaks had been replaced by lush green hills that eventually fell away to expose the water. With the aircraft close to the water, Laura could see numerous sleek speedboats as well as two old-fashioned clipper ships. *Two hundred years ago, all ships looked like that—creaky, dangerous, beautiful, white sails lit to gold by the afternoon sun.*

They landed with a large bump. Twenty minutes later, Laura emerged into the terminal. She rented a car and headed up Highway 101 toward San Francisco.

18

L aura had called on an old boyfriend for help. Jasper O'Shea was a cop, one of many reasons why their relationship had not lasted. Both knew that their friendship had evolved into something much more valuable than their sexual relationship had ever been. Jazz was now married with two children and was still a member of the same homicide division he'd been in fifteen years ago when they had met, he a rookie cop and she a Stanford undergraduate. As always, he had been delighted to hear from her and had taken the time to look up an old homicide case she was curious about.

After he had taken her to see an estate in the older, affluent part of town, she had invited him to dinner at a seaside restaurant, a favorite haunt from their past life together.

Jazz ordered a second Guinness and resumed the narrative.

"The case has never been solved. Luke Grimke was interviewed by the police on several occasions. He never cracked under the pressure and stuck firmly to his story that his wife was an insomniac and loved to paint in her studio at night."

He grabbed a piece of calamari and nodded in Laura's direction as he swallowed.

"You saw the property. The gate house where she painted is now connected to the house by a breezeway, but it wasn't back in 1979. No one could ever prove that Luke Grimke killed Julianna Grimke. The testimony of the orthopaedic surgeon and of the next-door neighbor who reported car headlights was just too convincing to the jury. They found reasonable doubt, and Grimke got off." Jazz shook his head. "Even the lie detector tests didn't help us; they were ruled as inadmissible. The guy was a defense lawyer's dream—precise, passionless, perfect."

Laura watched Jazz's face. He gazed back at her soberly.

"Between you and me, kid, the guy did it, no question. Couple months later, he collected life insurance, a cool million bucks, sold the house, sold his wife's gallery—that was another half a million—and headed out to the East Coast. Sounds like he's been on the straight and narrow ever since."

Laura raised her eyebrows. "Until now, perhaps?"

Jazz made a gesture denoting irrelevance. "Whatever, he can't be tried twice for the same crime." Laura watched his eyes light up as his porterhouse steak arrived. She had a final question before starting in on her grilled salmon.

"How was she killed, Jazz?"

"I thought I told you," he was chewing and gestured graphically with his steak knife. "She was stabbed in the heart."

By mutual unspoken consent, they spoke of other things during dinner and coffee and parted company close to midnight.

In her excitement over the new information, Laura did not sleep much. A pot of coffee kept her mind racing. The quaint bed and breakfast had a view of the water. She spent most of the night sitting on the balcony, listening to the surf and smelling the salty air as she reviewed the old newspaper clippings and the copy of the death certificate that Jazz had obtained for her.

Luke Grimke and Julianna Rydberg had met in Berkeley in 1976. She was already a well-known artist, with galleries in Monterey, San Francisco, and Sausalito. He had finished architecture school several years before. They married three months later, during the summer of the bicentennial. Laura gazed at a black and white reproduction of a newspaper wedding photo. She barely recognized Luke and was struck by how happy he looked, a smile transforming his features as he gazed at the woman next to him. She was looking directly into the camera, dark hair framing a heart-shaped face and serious eyes. Her lips were full with the corners tilting up in the barest of smiles. She looked, Laura realized, as if she were trying not to laugh.

The next few clippings were of various art exhibits and gallery openings. Laura saw that Julianna's work had been well-received. Mayors and even the governor had attended and bought her artwork. A well-known movie actor raved about her talent. She was quoted as finding her artistic rhythm at night "when nature sleeps, and inspiration finds solace in my nocturnal ways."

Luke's business, Pacific Rim Architecture, Inc., was also featured; in 1978, his was listed as the seventh wealthiest corporation in the Bay Area. An enthusiastic description of the Grimke estate dominated the Real Estate section of a July, 1978, newspaper. Laura recognized the Mediterranean exterior, complete with sweeping drive and porte-cochère. There were shots of the sunken pool —overlooking the San Francisco Bay— and a small, two-storied gate house peeking from the foliage beyond which a view of the sunset was visible.

This structure was featured heavily in the remaining newspaper clippings, all of which concerned Julianna's brutal murder in October, 1979, and its aftermath. Laura selected one of the shorter exposés and began to read.

The Bay Area was stunned by the news of the brutal murder of one of its brightest stars, artist Julianna Rydberg

Grimke, early this morning at her home in San Francisco. Mrs. Grimke's body was found this morning in her studio. A housekeeper discovered her face up in the remodeled gate house that she preferred for painting and noted extensive trauma to her thorax prior to summoning the Palo Alto police. "I did not attempt resuscitation because she was obviously dead," Maggie Cistern told police. 'Her hands were bloody, and there was a knife sticking out of her chest." Ms. Cistern does not remember open windows or other signs of forced entry. She recalls that the door to the gate house was unlocked when she noticed lights on shortly before seven o'clock and went to investigate. "It's not unusual for her to stay up most of the night painting, but she was almost always in bed by five. She told me she loved crawling into bed with her husband as the sun was about to come up."

The deceased is the wife of well-known architect, Lukas Grimke, who started Pacific Rim Architecture, Inc. six years ago. Its revenues have consistently been in the top five percent of Bay Area businesses. Mr. Grimke was not available for comment and has reportedly been staying at the home of a friend. It is said that he denies any knowledge of his wife's death, having been asleep on the second floor of their Mediterranean-style home between the hours of midnight and seven o'clock this morning when the police informed him of his wife's death.

"I thought he was going to lose it," reports a police officer who asks to remain anonymous. "He turned white as a sheet and didn't say a word after we told him." Grimke, who is currently using crutches because of a broken ankle, positively identified his wife's body before being taken to the police station for questioning. He was released to the care of his friend just over an hour later.

Several neighbors were also questioned. Abigail Barisch, whose property borders the southern edge of the Grimke estate, reports an uneventful night "except for headlights around 4 am. I know the car must have come down the driveway to the gate house, otherwise the lights wouldn't have swept over my walls. It's like a kaleidoscope, hard to sleep through. I didn't hear any noises, and I didn't notice the car leave. But my impression was that Juli had a visitor."

Other impressions of visitors allegedly include a coffee mug stained with a lipstick in a shade that Mrs. Grimke does not wear, according to her husband.

Police say that they have identified no definite suspects so far and urge anyone with knowledge that may be helpful to come forward.

Laura sighed and shuffled through the rest of the clippings. The obligatory shots of a body bag being removed from the premises made her sad. *To die is bad enough, but never to be avenged by identification of your killer is worse*, she decided. She read a small paragraph, dated several days later, with interest.

Police feel that they have enough evidence to justify the arrest of Lukas Grimke in the murder of his late wife, Julianna Rydberg Grimke. He will be arraigned on Friday. A February trial date is expected. Ms. Grimke died in her San Francisco home on October twelfth of penetrating trauma to the chest.

There was a great deal of paperwork about the trial, including a complete transcript of the entire event, which Laura was too tired to read. She would get to that later, along with the autopsy report.

Skipping to a report from the *San Francisco Observer* dated March, 1980, she found how the story ended.

In a stunning reversal in the courtroom today, lawyers for Lukas Grimke, the well-known architect whose trial for the October murder of his wife, Julianna Rydberg Grimke, has captured the attention of the Bay Area, presented evidence that he could not have stabbed his wife to death. They stated that his cast, placed below the knee for a broken left ankle two days prior to the murder was "pristine, without evidence of ambulation" when police asked the defendant to accompany them to the police station after informing him of his wife's death. Crutches were not found in the patient's bedroom.

Testimony by Mr. Grimke's orthopaedic surgeon, Dr. John Ridley, is scheduled for tomorrow in the San Francisco Superior Courthouse.

Mr. Grimke's lawyers say they expect a complete acquittal in the wake of this evidence.

The defendant himself has steadfastly maintained his innocence throughout the trial.

Laura put down the stack of papers and stretched. *I guess his lawyers were as good as their word,* she thought. *He got off.*

She felt her joints creak as she got up and moved through the French doors into the bathroom for a shower. A playful breeze across the bay rejuvenated her spirits as the dawn came; she made an early start, catching her connecting flight in Atlanta, and arriving in Charleston with just enough time to change into black and head to her second funeral that week.

* * * * *

That afternoon, Laura sat with Gigi at Brian's funeral. They were talking about the audacity of the crimes when

Gigi said: "I wonder who's making plans for the next funeral, Cleo's, I mean."

"I don't know," Laura said, not really caring. Her mind was fully engaged by the discoveries she had made at the offices of the San Francisco newspaper and the police department the day before.

Gigi kept talking. "I suppose she has family somewhere. All that information should be in her records with the firm. But the police must already know about next of kin because nobody asked me. I hope it's not that pothead boyfriend of hers."

Laura focused and tried to hide her surprise. "Luke's nephew is a drug addict?"

Gigi waved a hand impatiently as the organ music began, in a mournful déjà vu of the service they had attended forty-eight hours earlier. "No, this is some other guy. They'd been living together for months, common-law, maybe."

"Then what was she doing with...?" Laura let the thought remain unfinished. Maybe Cleo and her boyfriend had had a fight. Kyle was her way of making him sit up and pay attention.

Laura decided to have a talk with the boyfriend. She walked over to Pitt Street that afternoon, after the service.

* * * * *

The apartment that Joey Hamilton and Cleo Cooper shared was on the second floor of a grungy-looking house near the College of Charleston. The once-imposing home had been carved up into little units to accommodate the large student population that now inhabited the area west of King Street and east of Colonial Lake, which approximated the sprawling College of Charleston. The place was in dire need of a coat of paint and some landscaping. A surfboard was haphazardly flung into the entryway; trash cans were overflowing, mostly with pizza boxes and beer bottles. Apparently, no one had heard of recycling.

She rang the bell and was rewarded by the sound of a door opening upstairs and a shout.

"Yo, c'mon up!" The voice was baritone. Laura climbed the rickety staircase and saw a figure lounging in the doorway. She extended a hand.

"You must be Mr. Hamilton," she said, sympathetic in light of his recent loss. "I'm Laura Lindross, a friend of Cleo's." Laura felt bad about stretching the truth, but the boy seemed to take the explanation at face value. "I'm sorry for what happened."

"You can call me Joey." He shook Laura's hand as an apparent afterthought and seemed to find nothing odd about her arrival to talk to him. He motioned her inside.

She stepped over the threshold and was surprised at the place. It faced north and west, and golden sun was pouring into the large living room. A creative hand had worked hard to make the place seem like home. Although she was not sure, Laura guessed it was Cleo's work, now overlaid with a several-day layer of junk, whether due to habitual sloth or acute depression, she couldn't tell.

The wooden floor was polished and pastel chenille rugs were strewn about. One was round with gold stars and a big sun with wavy rays emanating outward. The northern wall was painted in a shimmery blue color; the fat gold stars painted on it reflected a shared motif. The sofa was old, but had been painstakingly slip-covered in cheerful red and white stripes. Jewel-tone goblets and dirty dishes were strewn about on every surface; the kitchen, windowless, was painted green. Plants were strategically placed, but beginning to wilt. She guessed that Joey was either unwilling or unable to perpetuate the cozy atmosphere that his girlfriend had worked so hard to create.

Laura sat on a plump chair next to a hand-painted coffee table that held a book entitled *Horoscope: Hidden Insight for a Happy Life* as well as multiple issues of Cosmopolitan and People magazine. A half-empty pack of cigarettes was visible under two empty pizza boxes and what looked suspiciously like a homemade bong.

In the kitchen, Joey held up a bottle of Bud. "Want one?"

Laura shook her head and wondered if he was going to offer her a hit from the bong next. She watched as he twisted the cap off the beer bottle and padded across the floor, lowering himself onto the sofa next to her. "So, whassup?" He did not look like a man incapacitated by grief, but one never knows.

Laura took a deep breath. "You may know that Cleo appears to have been attacked by someone who knew her. The police have reason to think that her death is linked to that of two other people, the architects she worked for. I wonder, Joey, if she ever mentioned anything unusual or interesting that happened at the office, something she overheard or knew about that might shed some light on the situation?"

Joey took a swig of beer. "No, there's nothin' really. The police spent half the damn day askin' me questions, too, while I was at work. You with them?" Laura thought she saw a gleam of respect in his eyes.

"No," she said reluctantly. "I'm just trying to figure out what's going on."

Conversation with Joey was not illuminating. He seemed apathetic. Laura guessed this was probably a side effect of the marijuana he habitually smoked. He did not seem torn up about his girlfriend's death, nor about the fact that she'd died while spending the night at another guy's house. She did not understand this, but realized that he was probably not indifferent. Everyone handled grief differently.

She was literally on her way out the door when Joey snapped his fingers. "Hey, almost forgot, Cleo did come home one day, about, maybe, two weeks ago, sayin' somethin' about who she worked for, was havin' an affair, or somethin' like that, and she didn't like it, neither."

"Who was having the affair, Joey?" Laura willed her hands to her sides and realized she was holding her breath.

"Well, I think it was the lady she worked for," Joey wrinkled up his forehead. "And the guy she worked for."

"Two of the architects were having affairs?" Laura was momentarily confused, then in a rush, understood. "With each other?"

"Yeah, I guess, I dunno," Joey's mental prowess was at an end. He cracked his knuckles and looked bored, starting to close the door behind her.

"Joey, come on, please try, can you remember anything else?"

He shrugged. "Well, gee, she was always goin' on about somethin', I never could keep track," he offered. "Always told her she was the original space case. I kinda miss that now." He sighed, then met her eyes, perhaps aware he was saving the best for last. "She did say that Leos are never successful with other Leos, some horoscope thing, ya know, she was real into that, they both want to be the dominant one, always tryin' to win. She said it would never work. That's why she disapproved."

Laura left the shabby building, heart pounding, cursing herself for being too snobby to carry a cell phone. She wanted to call Kate and ask her when Mark's birthday had been. As it was, she hurried back to Fort Sumter House and paged her friend. Two minutes later the telephone rang.

She seized the receiver like a drowning woman would a life preserver. "Kate!"

The voice at the other end was polite. Laura heard Jimmy Buffett in the background, singing about a woman being to blame. "Hi, this is Annette returning a page for Dr. Caxton. She's scrubbed in, may I take a message?"

Damn. Laura murmured a message for Kate to call her as soon as the emergency surgery was done, then dialed Melanie's house. She did not think Brian had been the one having the affair, but one never knows. Melanie answered on the second ring, sounding depressed.

"Chivas residence," she intoned.

Laura identified herself and decided to get to the point in a circuitous fashion, not wanting to tell the new widow the whole story. "How are you feeling?" The funeral had been hard for Melanie. She had cried the whole time, using Brian's brother's shoulder as a handkerchief.

"I'm better, Brad and Angie are staying for a few days, we'll get through. You're sweet to call, though."

Laura was wondering how to ask about Brian's birthday when she realized his birthdate was listed on the program from the church service she had just attended. She asked Melanie to call her if she needed anything and hung up, her sweaty fingers encountering the stiff white program in her blazer pocket. Why had she not thought of this before? And where was her program from Mark's service on Tuesday? The vital information was right in front of her nose, and she hadn't even seen it.

She brought the paper out and looked. On the front, in perfect, black script, was her answer. *Brian Gaston Chivas, born August 10, 1959.*

Laura's thoughts collided and shouted inside her head —Gigi and Brian! No wonder Melanie had been pissed. Had she known? Did this explain her venom about Kate's affair with Jimmy? You betrayed him, she had hissed. Was that a reflection of her feelings about Brian?

Laura took a deep breath. So. Gigi had gotten her hooks into Brian. What did that mean? How did that change what Laura already knew? Was the unsolved murder, so many years ago, of Luke's wife just a red herring? Maybe Melanie had a clearer motive now for killing her husband, but what about killing Mark? And where did Cleo fit in?

Laura rubbed her temples and poured a cup of coffee to assist in her thought process. The basic problem was that she could not imagine Melanie killing three people. But, as Agatha Christie said: *Every murderer is somebody's old friend.* One never knows.

Laura decided to go straight to the source. She picked up the telephone and dialed Gigi's number.

19

Gigi re-crossed her shapely legs and took another sip of wine. Late afternoon traffic was audible on East Bay Street through the lace-curtained windows of her drawing room.

"So I was having an affair with Brian. What's the big deal? I didn't kill him, and I didn't kill anyone else." She looked bored. "It would've ended soon anyway, he was wracked with guilt about Melanie, I guess he'd never cheated on her before, and he wasn't that great in the sack. But it was kind of fun to be doing it right under Mark's nose. He would've shit a brick if he'd known. He sometimes acted as if Brian should be asking his permission about everything." She sipped more wine and arched an eyebrow. "You know, they sure didn't see eye to eye about everything, not like some people think. In fact…"

Although they were seated in the privacy of her living room, Gigi leaned forward and lowered her voice. "In fact, last week, I think it was two weeks ago today, I heard Mark and Brian yelling, just yelling at each other, in the conference room. I don't know what it was about, but I'm surprised Cleo didn't hear it also; they were quite loud, and the conference room was right next to her desk." She broke off, and they stared at each other. Laura spoke first.

"Maybe she did hear," Laura sucked in her breath. "And maybe that's what got her killed."

Gigi was silent for a long moment, then shook her head. "I should have asked, or listened more, goddammit. There was something going on in the office, Laura, and I want to know what it was. Brian never said a word, but I think there was something really bothering him." She sounded frustrated as she got up and went into the kitchen. "More wine?" Laura saw that her refrigerator held green and red grapes, as well as Irish cheddar and fresh mozzarella.

"Sure, that'd be great." Laura followed her. "I can't remember the last time I ate." She was sitting down at the kitchen table when a corner of white paper, underneath one of the table's elegant claw-feet, caught her eye. It was the program from Mark's funeral. She stepped over and freed it, running her finger over the creamy parchment. On instinct, she opened it. *Marcus Michael Caxton, born July 29, 1959.*

Laura scrunched up her face. End of July, 1959. Mark and Brian were only a couple of weeks apart in age. She had not known that. Well, everyone always said they were very alike, told each other everything. And both were Leos!

Straightening slowly, she realized that everything had fallen into place. Kate had been right. Mark had been having an affair, not with Amanda, but with Gigi! No wonder he stopped talking about work and become increasingly distant. He was cheating with his colleague! He had a history of unchivalrous behavior with women, Laura remembered, and Kate was simply another disappointed woman.

But how disappointed was she? Laura slowly put down the program and reached for a grape. Did Kate kill him over it? Did Gigi, and if so, why? Laura thought of her promise to help her friend and turned to find Gigi watching her. The older woman's eyes were very bright.

"Laura? What's the matter?" Gigi carried her empty wineglass to the sink. "You look like you've seen a ghost."

Laura found that her mouth was inexplicably dry. "Were you having an affair with both of them, Gigi?" Laura continued, "What are you trying to prove? Being an adulteress isn't as bad as being a murderess, but I still think…"

Gigi put the glass down on the counter with such force that it cracked. Her voice was harsh. "Stop moralizing to me, you little saint! All you do is live in your escapist, story book little world! You don't know what it's been like for me! I never had anything to do with that weenie, Brian; it was Mark and I who knew we were going to be together. The first time we met, I felt he was different from anyone else I've ever been with. I've always had a great career and a bad personal life. Men are scared of me, I think; each new guy, I'd see the future in his eyes, things would be great, then he'd give me some stupid reason for leaving! I wanted kids, a husband, but they all treated me like a cheap fuck! I was about to turn forty, and I could've killed some of them, I was so tired of feeling that way!"

She seemed to realize what she had just said. Taking a deep breath, her face softened as she remembered. "Then I came down here, a new life, a new start, all because of Mark. It took me almost a year to get him into bed, but it was wonderful when it happened. He told me he loved me, was unable to fight his feelings anymore, thought I was beautiful, smart, worthwhile! The only bad thing was that he was really allergic to Max. But, he said he'd get a divorce. He said he'd bring it up with Kate. I was patient; I waited for almost another year. When he called me on Saturday morning, I thought that's what it was going to be about. I was so happy! I ran down to the store just to quickly peek at what they had, thinking we'd be furnishing our own home soon, then grabbed coffee at Starbucks and made Max wait while I hurried down to his house." Her eyes darkened. "Their house."

"I'd been there a couple other times and knew they kept it unlocked. I went in, his wife was at work; I didn't see any reason to knock. I knew he'd be in the study and went there. And that's when I saw him. He was lying there, wearing a white shirt, but it looked red with all the blood. I knew he was dead. I did nothing, just turned around and walked away." She looked down at her hands.

"Why didn't you call the police?" Laura asked gently. "You've just narrowed the time of death to between seven-fifteen and seven forty-five."

Gigi started to cry. "I don't know, it's just that they twist things so much. I was having an affair with him. I snuck down there at dawn, and I found him dead. They'd say that I had a reason for killing him."

"Did you?" Laura asked.

"No!" Gigi shouted the word. "I wanted him alive. He was my future. And now all that's left is the Jack Citrons of this world." She blew her nose, then spoke in a more modulated tone. "Truthfully? I thought Kate had done it. I thought he must have told her about me, and she lost it."

Laura considered. "She's the one person who couldn't have done it, you know. She was twenty minutes away, seeing patients at seven-thirty. She didn't have enough time, either before or after, to kill him."

Gigi rolled her eyes. "Maybe she killed him right before she left the house, and the medical examiner is a little bit off on the time."

Laura could not help but smile. She gave the older woman's hand a squeeze. "They're trained not to be 'a little bit off', Gigi. You found him dead at nearly seven-forty-five, right? It had to have been someone else. Come on, you worked with all three of the victims. You had to have seen something, or heard something. Think, think, think!"

Laura mentally chalked one up to Bill Sullivan, who must have seen Gigi, not Kate, entering the Lamont Street home at seven forty-five. Red hair, little black sweater, khakis, it was the epitome of autumnal casual wear in the southeast right now.

Thirty minutes later, the two women had gone over the events of the preceding week without uncovering any new information. Laura told Gigi about Julianna Grimke's twenty-year-old unsolved murder, but the other woman was unsurprised. Luke had told her everything the previous day at lunch.

"He told you all that?" Laura could not believe it.

Gigi smiled, a small, secretive smile. "The man is worried about something. I think he knows whom he doesn't want as an enemy. I think he thought that maybe I already knew about his wife."

"Did you?"

"Of course not, Laura, where would I get information like that, and why would I care?"

Laura considered this. She thought about revealing the other new wrinkle in the case, Kate's affair with Jimmy and her pregnancy, but loyalty to her friend kept her from sharing this. After a while, the women made coffee, and Laura was reminded of a last question. "Did you notice a coffee cup in the study when you found Mark? I saw a large one broken on the floor, with an identical one sitting in the kitchen, unused."

Gigi nodded. "Yes, It must have dropped from his hands as he was stabbed. But I was never in the kitchen so I don't know what he had in there." Her green eyes widened. "Maybe he was expecting someone that morning who wasn't a coffee drinker, but he didn't know that."

Laura felt her heart plummet as she met Gigi's gaze. They spoke simultaneously, "Amanda."

* * * * *

Forging an alliance of necessity, Laura and Gigi decided to question Amanda in a public place, in case their inquiries resulted in a confession of murder. The three women agreed to meet for an early dinner at Magnolia's. The meal was uneventful until the dessert menus were delivered.

"I'll just have coffee," Gigi informed the waiter. Laura marveled at how good an actress she was. She had used her considerable social charms to put Amanda at ease during the meal and was now moving in for the kill. "Double espresso would be great. Amanda, how about you?"

Amanda's brown eyes were regretful. "No coffee for me, thanks; I've given it up, unfortunately." She smiled up at their server. "I'll have two scoops of the passion fruit sorbet, please." After Laura had ordered black coffee and the server had disappeared with the menus into the kitchen, she confided: "I've learned to satisfy my caffeine craving with sugar consumption."

"Why'd you give up coffee?" Gigi's voice was casual.

"Oh, you know, I was getting an irregular heartbeat with caffeine. It made me short of breath; my chest hurt." She shook her head. "You know, when something starts to threaten your health, you look at it a different way. I've been doing great without it for several years now."

"I get chest pains sometimes when I'm stressed," Gigi commented. "Maybe the palpitations were related to anxiety. Were you going through a difficult time when all that happened?"

Amanda appeared about to deny this, but then seemed to change her mind in mid-thought. "Yes, actually, I gave it up shortly after Mark broke up with me. We both used to drink pots of it, especially in the morning. I got the worst withdrawal headaches when I stopped drinking it; it's like

I was punishing myself for ever dating a jerk like him." She grimaced, then raised her eyebrows. "It's funny, I don't miss it at all now."

Gigi did not meet her eyes. "Amanda, the police might find all this interesting. Did you know that, the morning Mark died, he was expecting someone, a coffee drinker? He never knew you had given it up, did he?"

Laura thought Amanda looked confused, apparently not sure where Gigi was going with this. "No, I guess not."

Gigi's voice was very gentle. "You killed him, didn't you? You couldn't stand it anymore. A true crime of passion, you know that's manslaughter, not murder, right?" She looked at Amanda's blank face. "We'll come with you, honey; it's the right thing to do, to confess."

Laura squirmed in her chair, unable to meet Amanda's eyes and was shocked when Amanda giggled.

"The police already know." Her eyes shone with pleasure. "Girls, don't tell anyone, but I'm seeing Jeff, I mean, Detective Marcus."

Laura sat in stunned silence.

"Isn't that convenient?" Gigi offered, not missing a beat.

Amanda didn't notice Gigi's comment. "He's a sweetheart, but just separated. It's so new, we weren't going to tell anyone for quite a while. Not even his partner knows."

"Maybe this means you are ready to move on from Mark," Laura observed, recovering herself.

"Like she has a choice," Gigi added under her breath.

Again, it appeared as if Amanda was ignoring Gigi's snippy tone. She clearly wasn't going to let anyone take away the little happiness she had recently found. "We realize it's a conflict of interest, him being an investigating officer on the case. For a while I thought he was going to leave because of that, but everything's okay now. Thank God."

Laura could tell Amanda was genuinely relieved. "I guess it's good for you to have someone to help you through this difficult time." She looked to Gigi for agreement, but Gigi's impassive gaze told everyone she was no longer interested in the discussion.

"I don't know what I'd do without him right now," Amanda continued. "We talked about everything on Saturday; I was just miserable after that, until he decided yesterday he couldn't leave me. And he knows I didn't do it because he was with me on Saturday morning. That's why I was late to the gallery." She laughed again. "How's that for a cast-iron alibi?"

* * * * *

Laura paced, too disgruntled even to enjoy the view off her balcony. She was back to square one. No real suspects, no real plot. She realized that, in her novels, she had never done justice to the frustrations that the detective must experience. She usually picked the least likely suspect as the killer.

If she were writing a book about this experience, whom would she settle on as the murderer? Laura abruptly stopped pacing. *Of course, it's so obvious.* She grabbed her coat and left the apartment.

* * * * *

Jimmy Marin, wearing jailhouse orange, sat behind the plastic divider and held the telephone up to his ear. Laura saw his mouth move; his disembodied voice was released into her ear. He appeared calm and was very polite.

"I wish I could help you, but I didn't do it. I may not

have alibis like the other folks, but I didn't do it. My buddy, Tom Braden, he can vouch for me on Monday night, if that helps." Jimmy glanced around the fishbowl room he found himself in. "These guys'll figure it out. I'm innocent; I'm not worried. And Kate and I are gonna have a great future together."

Laura gazed at him. He seemed awfully sure of himself. For a moment, she saw what had attracted Kate. He was a wise young man, had barely shaken off the dew of adolescence for the mantle of manhood, but already carried it well. His prison garb did little to disguise his muscular arms; Laura pictured Kate burying her face in his furry chest. His gentle, sea-colored eyes watched her, encouraged her, and she heard herself say: "So you know about the baby?"

For a moment he was silent, then he grinned, a slow smile that removed him into his own little world. "She's pregnant, isn't she?" His eyes met Laura's. "I knew there was something she wasn't telling me." He gently rested his hands, palms down, on the table. "I'll take the greatest care of her. We'll have a child. We'll be a family. As soon as I get out of here." He smiled at Laura. "Don't worry about me, I couldn't be more happy. I can't believe she didn't tell me!"

Laura left him, still grinning and shaking his head, and felt guilty for having delivered Kate's exciting news to the new father of all people! She had been the only one trusted with the information, and now she had blown it. Kate would be very upset with her. She would know it was her fault. No one else knew about the baby.

Did they?

20

*S*o, *that's a wash,* Laura thought, as she left the Charleston County Correctional Facility. *He says he didn't do it, and I believe him. He's the obvious person to kill Mark, but I can't think of any reason for him to get rid of the other two.*

She drove south down Lockwood Boulevard past the marina. This stretch of road had recently been rejuvenated with strategically-placed palmetto trees and a new promenade, although the shipyard at the old coast guard station remained something of an eyesore.

Except on foggy nights, then it's like something out of a movie...This whole town is like that!

After a couple of race car curves, the shipyard came into view; the road narrowed into one lane, swooped to the left, and became the western end of Broad Street. Laura drove east, half-way down Broad, then, on an impulse, turned right, into the shady seclusion of Legare Street. Crossing Tradd, she continued toward South Battery, admiring, as she always did, the solid, stone homes on this reputedly most haunted street in Charleston. A block short of South Battery, she pulled over and eyed the house on her left. Its monolithic exterior was close to the street. As she got out of the car, she had to crane her neck to see its top floor. A single light shone up there, signifying to Laura that, perhaps, Luke Grimke was at home.

Laura crossed the street and climbed the steep marble stairs. After unsuccessfully looking for a doorbell, she lifted the brass lion's head knocker and let it fall once against the heavy oak door.

Luke answered the door himself, which, somehow, surprised Laura. He was wearing a pink dress shirt, unbuttoned at the top, without a tie, and his face looked a little pale underneath his tan. He looked worried, but the vertical lines at the sides of his mouth eased a bit when he saw Laura. He smiled and extended a large hand.

"Hi, Laura," his spontaneous use of her first name fit in with the expression of relief on his face. "Looks like we're neighbors. Come on in, can I get you a drink?" He led her through the dining room toward the kitchen; the two rooms were separated by a tastefully ornamental wet bar crafted of dark mahogany and replete with plenty of bottles and glassware. After pouring her a glass of zinfandel and refilling his lowball, they went up four flights of elegant staircase, emerging onto a rooftop terrace with a spectacular view of the water to the east, south, and west.

Laura made the appropriate exclamations of delight; Luke seemed pleased by her compliments. They kept the conversation light until they had both settled on chaises and remarked over the gray thunderclouds rolling in from the western sky. Then Luke abruptly finished his drink, put the glass down, and settled his gaze on Laura.

"We're both adults here," he remarked. "Much as I would like to think you've just dropped by for some southern hospitality and neighborly chitchat, I think you've probably got some questions for me that you want answered. That seems to be the trend around here lately."

Laura wondered briefly who else had been asking and nodded her head. Making sure she was between him and the door, she decided honesty was the best policy. "Luke, I appreciate your willingness to humor me. I guess the past few days have forced all of us to examine our souls and to try to get into each other's psyches as much as possible. I, as you may know, am a mystery novelist, and, as such, I tend to dig a bit more than most people." She met his gaze directly. "Luke, I know about Julianna. Is that episode in any way connected to this?"

She watched his face closely as she said his former wife's name, but he showed no emotion. His features instead assumed an expression that looked a lot like resignation. Raising his arms above his head, he did a neck roll or two, then settled his arms behind his head and unflinchingly returned her gaze.

"Your inquiry isn't original," he said dryly. "Whatever anonymity I've enjoyed these last twenty years will vanish when the newspaper gets ahold of this." He sighed. "I had nothing to do with Julianna's murder. To this day, there are no suspects. Yes, it bugs me, and, yes, it worries me a little because people will talk, but in the end, I'm okay because my conscience is clear and the people whose opinions I value know I had nothing to do with Julianna's death. Or with this mess out here." He grimaced, then smiled. "I guess I don't have anything to hide. What else do you want to know?"

Laura frowned. He was not behaving like a character in one of her books. She fumbled for her next question. "Where were you on Saturday morning, Sunday evening, and Monday night?"

He grinned. "You mean, what alibi do I have for each murder? Saturday at seven-thirty I was jogging. I went down to South Battery, ran west, looped around to the Battery, followed it east to White Point Gardens." He nodded at her. "Went right past your place, in fact. Always admire how that white stucco looks fresh-scrubbed in the morning sun. Then looped around to Tradd, took a right up Church as far as the Market, came down King and west on Tradd. Walked that last bit to cool down. Always do that. Didn't get near Lamont, fortunately. Or unfortunately, depends on how you look at it, I guess. Might've seen or heard something, or prevented Mark from his destiny." He shook his head. "Whatever, too late to dwell on it now. Sunday I was out to dinner at Peninsula Grill with a prospective partner over from Atlanta, gave the police his name already. We finished near nine o'clock, and, after I got my car back from the valet —I swear they drive my Jag for kicks— I drove past the Teeter thinking I'd pick up some cigars from their humidor, but the place was crawling with cops; I decided to avoid the place. Brings back too many memories."

Laura suddenly felt sorry for this middle-aged man sitting across from her with the black storm clouds forming behind him. He had dealt with more unhappiness in life than most people she knew. She looked at her hands, suddenly feeling guilty.

Luke continued. "And Monday I was with Veronica, got home around midnight, spent some time reading in the study, then hit the hay around two in the morning. Haven't been sleeping that well lately."

"I guess none of us have," Laura said softly. She reached out a hand. "Luke, I'm sorry..."

He grinned at her again; Laura remembered Kate's description: *smooth, sexy, sweet.* His charm was certainly working on her. Luke seemed to sense this and got up, taking her hand and tucking it companionably under his arm. "C'mon, you want a tour of the house? Cost me enough to re-vamp the place, I might as well show it off!"

Smiling down at her, he led the way to the door.

* * * * *

Thirty minutes later, Laura came home to find Gigi waiting outside Fort Sumter House for her, seeking shelter under its green canopy. It was getting dark, and the rain that had initially made small wet flecks on the pavement was now coming down in earnest.

"We were just taking a walk when the downpour started," Gigi offered, nodding at Max, who sat on his haunches, panting happily.

"That's good timing," Laura said, running her fingers through Max's damp fur. "Come on up, we can talk a little." She was happy to have an opportunity to relay her conversation with Luke and to put off the inevitable telephone call to Kate about her visit with Jimmy.

"So, I just got back from talking to Luke," Laura explained as they entered the condo, "and he insists he had nothing to do with his wife's murder or these murders here."

Gigi slowly nodded, settling into an armchair and absentmindedly stroking Max.

"Can I get you anything?" Laura called from the kitchen.

Gigi declined. "I've eaten so much today, I couldn't swallow a bite more. I can't even think straight about the murders anymore."

"Well, we're running out of suspects, Gigi," Laura sighed, as she collapsed onto the couch with an orange. "Amanda's cleared. I honestly don't think Melanie could've done it, and I think I believe Luke."

Her legs curled demurely under her, Gigi looked at Laura. "Everyone supposedly has her breaking point. Laura, what could make you kill someone?"

Laura was silent for a moment. "Well, I guess I could kill in self-defense, if I had to. And Kate told me once that, as a physician, she'd jump right in there to help anyone who was in trouble, even a complete stranger. She said it was her job, and she couldn't just stand by. Apathy breeds only apathy."

Gigi played with an auburn curl and spoke thoughtfully. "Yeah, I can see that. And I also think if l had children, and someone threatened them, I could kill, to end that threat. I bet that's something Kate's thinking about, too, especially now."

She looked up. "I guess you never know what you're truly capable of until it comes knocking on your door."

Laura grew aware of faint alarm bells going off in her head. "How did you know she was pregnant?"

Gigi spoke slowly. "Mark told me." She shrugged, then laughed suddenly. "That's the funny part. She hadn't even told him. He found a positive test in the trash and figured she was saving the information as a happy surprise for later." Her gaze was pinned on Laura's face. "That was his big news on Saturday morning! Yes, he was alive when I got there."

Laura couldn't believe the transformation of the woman in front of her. Gigi's normally polished features were suddenly transformed into a maniacal mask.

"Who did he think he was, that bastard? I couldn't believe it when he told me!" She raged, now out of the chair and pacing across the room. "She was pregnant, and he was going to do the right thing, break it off with me and be the best husband and father he could. He hoped I'd be happy for them and would continue to work at the firm and was sorry, but he didn't ever want her to know he'd strayed." Gigi rolled her eyes in disbelief. "He was sorry! Can you fucking believe it?"

"What happened next, Gigi?" Laura tried to keep her voice soft, not wanting to provoke her further. The alarm bells were very loud now.

Gigi turned toward Laura, eyes locking on hers. "Next? Do I have to spell it out for you? Don't you make your living plotting these things?" The accusation was sarcastic. "I killed him, of course! Sorry I lied to you earlier, but what did you think? Yes, he was alive when I got there and dead when I left." Her voice held an undercurrent of pride. "You know, I surprised myself even more than I surprised him. Never knew I had it in me. I used a very sharp ornamental letter opener that was on his desk. He barely knew what happened, dropped his coffee cup, fell back, collapsed on the desk. There wasn't even much blood at first." Gigi's cheeks flushed as she remembered. "Believe me, I wanted to watch him die, but I had to get out of there. Max was tied up outside Metropolitan. I was lucky no one saw me leave. I've always been lucky that way. The salesgirl thought I was at Starbucks the whole time. It took less than ten minutes." She seemed to remember her former train of thought. "Yes, it would have given me great pleasure to watch Mark die. Best relationship I was ever in, and he wanted to leave me for a baby!"

Laura was paralyzed with fear and asked about the first thing that came into her head to keep Gigi talking. "Did he offer coffee?"

Gigi looked confused for a moment, then her eyes cleared. "I already had my coffee from Starbucks, so I didn't need his. But he did offer it. You saw the matching mug in the kitchen, I forgot." She advanced toward Laura and asked scornfully, "What else can I tell you to help the pieces fall into place?"

Laura spoke more out of desperation than to know the complete answer to the puzzle. "And Brian, Cleo? Why'd you kill them?"

Gigi sighed. "Mark told Brian everything; he was the only one who knew about us. I knew he'd tell the cops eventually. I had to get my hands on him as soon as he got off that airplane. Melanie told me they'd be at the Harris Teeter. I knew what time the flight came in, so I put Max into the car and waited. I live so close; it was pretty easy, but I was more scared. There was more blood, but I had my raincoat on, and all the blood got washed away in the pouring rain. Again I was lucky! A perfect night for murder."

Her mouth curved into a triumphant half-smile, but a moment later Laura saw her eyes cloud up.

"But, poor Max, I think he knew something was going on. He thinks I'm the greatest, but, that night, he knew I'd done something bad; he whined all the way out to Folly, acted scared of me. It almost broke my heart." Her voice became businesslike. "As for Cleo, I strangled the little slut because she figured it out and tried to blackmail me. Called me on her cell phone from some bar and told me to meet her at Luke Grimke's beach house at midnight. Was all sure of herself, just because she was gonna get laid by some little rich kid. Wanted to be rich herself. I had the five grand, and I strangled her so Max wouldn't smell the blood. He loves me so much. I didn't want to disappoint him."

Laura gambled again, wishing Gigi were not standing between her and the door. "It wasn't even his, the baby, did you know that? Kate was involved with somebody else too! Gigi, once that information comes out, no one will ever suspect you. It would look as if you killed him for nothing."

Gigi froze. Slowly, she placed a hand over her heart, bending a little at the waist as if in physical pain. For a moment, Laura thought she might throw up or crumple to the ground. Then she spoke, her voice a malevolent hiss. "Don't you dare tell me I killed him for nothing, you bitch! It isn't true, it isn't!" Her voice rose in despair and rage. "Don't you lie to me! You're lying!" She charged quickly, but Laura was faster. She ran out onto the balcony.

Don't look down.

Gigi followed more slowly, her silhouette black in the doorway. "Max is waiting, so no blood." She almost seemed to be talking to herself. In the next moment, however, her voice vibrated with contempt. "You think you're so smart, writing about murder. Well, I think you will have to admit that experiencing it is a different story." She stepped onto the white marble; a large ring on her left hand flashed as it reflected light from the kitchen.

Laura felt time slow down as she looked into the bright emerald eyes of a killer. Then the woman was upon her, barely giving her time to turn and escape grasping hands. She was less than a foot from the wrought iron balcony rail with nowhere to go.

She jumped.

Epilogue

T here is a little westward curve in Church Street, right where St. Philip's Church is. After living in Charleston for over a year, Laura knew the beautiful street by heart.

Entering the crowded church, she gripped Tag's hand more tightly. John Tagliani had taken a few days off from his job as an editor in New York City to accompany her to the wedding of one of her best friends. His arm offered physical as well as emotional support, since she still limped a little after sustaining a comminuted fracture of the left leg and a shattered pelvis as a result of her fall the previous September. Tag had cared for her then, too, confessing later that, as she lay in a coma for two days after falling forty feet, he had not been sure she would survive. A fortuitously placed palmetto tree had served to break her fall a little bit, perhaps saving her life.

How long ago it all seems, Laura thought, as they surveyed the golden interior of the church.

On this glorious autumn day the sun was shining, and the humidity that characterizes Low Country summers was gone. Pale pink roses were demure in the late afternoon sunlight. The hushed conversation of family and friends surrounding her was the only sound.

Tag led her to a pew near the front, where Kate was already sitting. She was dressed in a sweep of bold summer green that brought out the red in her hair and that of the baby in the arms of the man next to her. Jimmy was wearing a dark suit and looked every inch the adoring father. As Laura watched, he leaned over and kissed Kate's lips, then caught sight of Laura and waved her over, an eager smile on his face.

It all turned out so great for them.

"How's the baby?" Laura asked, as Kate turned to her with shining eyes. "I can't believe she's already four months old!"

The organ music finally began; a little boy near the front of the church started to sing along in a high, happy voice. "Here comes the bride, big, fat, and wide." Words turned into squeals as his father muffled the sound with a large hand, and several guests laughed.

Amanda did not look any of those things as she appeared in the doorway. She looked radiant, with her mother on one side and her father on the other. Her eyes were fixated on the man standing at the front of the church next to the minister.

Laura sighed and turned to gaze at the maid of honor, who caught her eye almost immediately and smiled. Melanie looked happy and healthy in her pink slip dress. *She doesn't talk about Brian much anymore*, Laura realized.

Instead, Melanie had thrown herself into her gallery and loved to spend quiet evenings at home with Domino, painting in her studio and trusting herself to be happy once again. She had sold several paintings on the opening night of her last exhibit and had recently confessed to Laura that she felt more confident of a peaceful future than ever before. *Good things never come easy*, she had said.

That's true, Laura thought and squeezed Tag's arm. She felt lucky to have him. He understood her, had already stood by her in sickness and in health. He cared about her spirit, her dreams, her nightmares.

She spoke softly into his ear. "Doesn't it all seem so far away now? Gigi wanted exactly what you and I have, respect for each other, a future together." She reached for his hand. "You know, sometimes I still dream about a black-hooded figure moving along the Battery with that snowy white dog dancing, prancing in her wake, smiling. And not a day goes by when I don't ponder the volatility of human emotion and the paradox of the human heart."

At the front of the church, Amanda took Detective Jeff Marcus's hand, and the ceremony began.

Other Savage Press Books

OUTDOORS, SPORTS & RECREATION

Cool Fishing for Kids 8-85 by Frankie Paull and "Jackpine" Bob Cary
Curling Superiority! by John Gidley
Dan's Dirty Dozen by Mike Savage
The Duluth Tour Book by Jeff Cornelius
The Final Buzzer by Chris Russell

ESSAY

Battlenotes: Music of the Vietnam War by Lee Andresen
Hint of Frost, Essays on the Earth by Rusty King
Hometown Wisconsin by Marshall J. Cook
Potpourri From Kettle Land by Irene I. Luethge

FICTION

Burn Baby Burn by Mike Savage
Charleston Red by Sarah Galchus
Keeper of the Town by Don Cameron
Lake Effect by Mike Savage
Mindset by Enrico Bostone
Off Season by Marshall J.Cook
Something in the Water by Mike Savage
The Year of the Buffalo by Marshall J. Cook
Voices From the North Edge by St. Croix Writers
Walkers in the Mist by Hollis D. Normand

REGIONAL HISTORY, HUMOR, MEMOIR

Beyond the Freeway by Peter J. Benzoni
Crocodile Tears and Lipstick Smears by Fran Gabino
Fair Game by Fran Gabino
Some Things You Never Forget by Clem Miller
Stop in the Name of the Law by Alex O'Kash
Superior Catholics by Cheney and Meronek
Widow of the Waves by Bev Jamison

BUSINESS

Dare to Kiss the Frog by vanHauen, Kastberg & Soden
SoundBites Second Edition by Kathy Kerchner

POETRY

Appalachian Mettle by Paul Bennett
Eraser's Edge by Phil Sneve
Gleanings from the Hillsides by E.M. Johnson
In the Heart of the Forest by Diana Randolph
Moments Beautiful Moments Bright by Brett Bartholomaus
Nameless by Charlie Buckley
Pathways by Mary B. Wadzinski
Philosophical Poems by E.M. Johnson
Poems of Faith and Inspiration by E.M. Johnson
The Morning After the Night She Fell Into the Gorge by Heidi Howes
Thicker Than Water by Hazel Sangster
Treasured Thoughts by Sierra
Treasures from the Beginning of the World by Jeff Lewis

SOCIAL JUSTICE

Throwaway People: Danger in Paradise by Peter Opack

SPIRITUALITY

Life's Most Relevant Reality by Rod Kissinger, S.J.
Proverbs for the Family by Lynda Savage, M.S.
The Awakening of the Heart by Jill Downs
The Hillside Story by Pastor Thor Sorenson

OTHER BOOKS AVAILABLE FROM SP

Blueberry Summers by Lawrence Berube
Beyond the Law by Alex O'Kash
Dakota Brave by Howard Johnson
Jackpine Savages by Frank Larson
Spindrift Anthology by The Tarpon Springs Writer's Group
The Brule River, A Guide's Story by Lawrence Berube
Waterfront by Alex O'Kash

To order additional copies of

Charleston Red

or to
receive a copy of the complete
Savage Press Catalog,
contact us at:

Local calls:
(Superior, WI/Duluth, MN area)
715-394-9513

National Voice and FAX orders
1-800-732-3867
E-mail:
mail@savpress.com

Visit on-line at:

www.savpress.com

Visa/MasterCard Accepted

All Savage Press books are available at all chain and
independent bookstores nationwide. Just ask them to
special order if the title is not in stock.